A CYLINDRICAL OBJECT ON FIRE IN THE DARK

A CYLINDRICAL OBJECT ON FIRE IN THE DARK

Holly Myers

INSERT
BLANC
PRESS

Los Angeles

A version of "Istanbul" first appeared in *Joyland*, April 2009.

"The Guest Room" first appeared in *ZZYZZYVA*, Fall 2010. It was reprinted in *New California Writing 2012*, Heyday Books (2012).

"My Arrival" first appeared in *Antioch Review*, Spring 2015.

Front and Back Cover photography courtesy of Liza Ryan.

For Tom.

CONTENTS

PART I

Choices

1

So, what are we going to do?

Life is full of choices.

Yes, but this is one choice. Just one.

One way or another.

Exactly.

But it's not like the world stops, you know. It doesn't really matter.

Don't you be getting all philosophical.

Like, did you see that thing?

What thing?

Up at the top of the building.

What are you talking about?

I don't know, it was this big thing. I don't know. Round. That someone built.

On the top of a building?

Downtown.

What does that have to do with anything?

2

I didn't feel well.

Last night?

Right.

I'm not saying that he had any problem.

I know.

He didn't say anything to me.

I know. I'm just saying I didn't feel well. It was not an experience of *wellness* exactly. Watching that.

What, because of who was there?

No, it was me. I have been thinking we need a wider way of talking about all these ways that we go on being. All these things, you know, that jump around.

So what did you feel when he spoke?

Oh, I don't know. It's not that. It's not him speaking exactly.

You didn't mind that?

It's not a matter of whether I minded. Though yes, you're right. There is something about his voice, in a way. But that wasn't really the pressing thing.

What was the pressing thing?

Well, there were all these tables, right? And plates. But his voice—you're right, actually. Now that I think about it. There is this little, I don't know what you'd call it. This note in there, like a little squeak.

But what were you *feeling?*

Well, so you know, if wellness is that feeling of just filling the container and everything's smooth and no sloshing around, even when you move from one place to another?

Yes.

Well, that is what I didn't feel.

Fragments

there was the yawning of a dangerous emptiness
filled with bird sounds
and wind chimes

*

she does *would you like peanuts*
when she's drunk
perfect
and the table roars with laughter

she does it in her sleep
she does it without irony

*

to cross beaches gathering bullet casings
and old tin cans and stones

to stand—not be—without meaning or need—looking closely

*

it is simple like death must be:
the mind flickers, slips, and regains itself
the mind flickers, slips, and out

*

can't help looking in mirrors
dodges the onset of solitude
needs of—herself
needs of—the glowing gaze to draw her contours
and keep her bound inside her skin

he speaks with the fever of yes and
                              what luck

one

one who moves slowly one who always brings flowers one who speaks before she thinks one who is in the habit of regretting one who turns every light off twice one who hears music vividly one who follows politics one who taps his foot habitually one who covets new technologies one who hates his father one who is always a little afraid of driving one who sighs without realizing it one who looks much younger than she is one who subscribes to seven magazines one who wears red often one who remembers palm trees in childhood one who loves beets one who would have died for a tree house one who can't shake the sense of being followed one who relaxes when the lights go off one who keeps a bowl of hard wrapped candies one who frequently enters contests one who loses his temper easily one who needs a lot of love one who is only happy in summer one who feels confident wearing a tie one whose father was a forest ranger one who is overwhelmed in grocery stores one who has once been electrocuted one who visits her mother weekly one who sees nothing wrong with farting one who can't fall asleep before three a.m. one who takes pleasure in hardware stores one who looks stately when silent one who feels most alive at a party one who hates the sight of his feet one who has unusually violent dreams one who tips quickly from arrogance to despair one who always buys the same kind of socks one who tends to drink his first drink quickly one who finds it difficult to curse one who misses adolescent romance one who believes he is allergic to plums one who desires only uneducated women one who is haunted by what she's never told her sister one who secretly prefers fast food one who looks at his son with dismay one who buys only expensive pens one who knows that she's good at selling things one who takes pleasure envisioning his wife with others one who's never been afraid of dying one who was beautiful only in youth one whose voice tends to rise above all others one who feels most comfortable with children one who has seen another murdered one who is trying to learn how to listen one who is sick at the thought of gin one who is fundamentally surprised by tragedy one who is nervous to be alone on the highway one who picks up languages quickly one

15

who reveals himself only to strangers one who sees it as her duty to be cheerful one whose impulse is often to flee one who has contemplated committing a serious crime one who enjoys the feeling of hardiness in winter one who gives love desperately one who longs sincerely for the presence of God one who travels more than he is ever at home

Fragments

the wind came for you
and the bird whose flutter madness was golden in the light
and the color slipped off otherwise

*

how the plaster creeps across our skin—
his age turned to liquid trembles

she is hard, she is German, an actress
her face is a dorm room
covered in moss

they stay the world with their
entitlement
each word has a belly of water

*

the low rumbling of argument, crisis,
little peaks of force and exasperation
the ebb of fatigue
turning circles again and again
the baby cries

worn down by constant association

*

the clouds pass hugely here
gathering then releasing
the flood weight of the sun

Primary Emotions

Fear
A woman outside a gas station in Needles, California. It is 102 degrees. There is a patch of grass to the side of the air compressor and a soiled paper napkin laying on the grass. She carries a purse and an empty plastic bottle.

Joy
A woman alone in a car at 82 miles per hour, 46 miles west of Elko, Nevada, 11 a.m. on a Tuesday.

Trust
A woman in a car with two young children in the third lane from the right on Interstate 10, south Phoenix. Traffic is tight but moving. She's digging in her purse for a phone that is ringing.

Surprise
A woman pulled from a car that has overturned to the side of a long, flat road north of Laramie, Wyoming. It's late at night; the headlights tip upward.

Sadness
A woman and a man in a car outside a diner in Durango. The snow has been largely cleared from the roads but is piled nearly four feet high on the sidewalks.

Disgust
A woman alone in a car at a stoplight in Albuquerque. A man outside does something with his tongue.

Anger
A woman reaches 57 miles per hour on a two-block span between red lights—Beverly Boulevard, Koreatown, Los Angeles. It is 10:46 p.m. The man in the car says nothing.

Anticipation
A woman in a car with a backpack in the trunk, a motel parking lot, Columbia Falls, Montana.

She / He

She opened the box.
She shattered the glass.
She measured the flour.
She took off the hat.
She polished the frame.
She turned on the faucet.
She shelved the book.
She pulled the shades.
She fixed the drawer.
She lit the candle.
She emptied the jar.
She dropped the plate.
She sat on the step.
She reached for the keys.
She shook the bottle.
She crumpled the napkin.
She waved the envelope.
She mended the sweater.
She closed the oven.
She lowered the camera.
She rinsed the glass.
She locked the door.
She opened the window.

He closed the window.
He answered the door.
He dropped the wrench.
He cleared the shelves.
He moved the chair.
He fanned the fire.
He watered the plant.
He changed the clock.
He started the car.
He called the dog.
He tossed the magazine.
He shed the jacket.
He shouldered the bag.
He turned down the music.
He folded the tablecloth.
He threw the pillow.
He replaced the spoon.
He turned the page.
He examined the cuff.
He straightened the sheet.
He leaned on the bannister.
He raised the glass.
He closed the box.

She closed the window.
She answered the door.
She dropped the wrench.
She cleared the shelves.
She moved the chair.
She fanned the fire.
She watered the plant.
She changed the clock.
She started the car.
She called the dog.
She tossed the magazine.
She shed the jacket.
She shouldered the bag.
She turned down the music.
She folded the tablecloth.
She threw the pillow.
She replaced the spoon.
She turned the page.
She examined the cuff.
She straightened the sheet.
She leaned on the bannister.
She raised the glass.
She closed the box.

He opened the box.
He shattered the glass.
He measured the flour.
He took off the hat.
He polished the frame.
He turned on the faucet.
He shelved the book
He pulled the shades.
He fixed the drawer.
He lit the candle.
He emptied the jar.
He dropped the plate.
He sat on the step.
He reached for the keys.
He shook the bottle.
He crumpled the napkin.
He waved the envelope.
He mended the sweater.
He closed the oven.
He lowered the camera.
He rinsed the glass.
He locked the door.
He opened the window.

to be as

to be as one cheated to be as one gifted to be as one vexed to be
as one ebullient to be as one at fault to be as one needed to be as
one short of breath to be as one cajoled to be as one dizzy with
happiness to be as one at sea to be as one enraged to be as one
full of feeling to be as one stricken by unwanted knowledge to
be as one in a state of grace to be as one temporarily exempted
to be as one accomplished in chess to be as one wondered at
to be as one whose glory has faded to be as one slaphappy to
be as one unnerved by argument to be as one coveted to be as
one of low ambition to be as one caged to be as one conceded
to to be as one enlightened early in life to be as one contained
to be as one on the edge to be as one colluded against to be as
one triggered to be as one collapsed at the center to be as one
already launched to be as one shrunken to be as one expended
to be as one doomed to be as one perpetually warmed by the sun
to be as one whose language is polished to be as one who was
beaten as a child to be as one forborne to be as one sterilized to
be as one frequently rewarded to be as one shaken to be as one
well trained to be as one who is wont to shut down to be as one
contented to be as one accustomed to be as one expensively fed
to be as one exceptional to be as one all too easily grasped to be
as one who has fled to be as one entitled to be as one enraptured
to be as one patronized to be as one in doubt to be as one livid
to be as one forcibly compelled to be as one pitied to be as one
naïve to be as one outstretched to be as one discarded to be as
one in motion to be as one bejeweled to be as one just caught to
be as one persuaded to be as one heavily made up to be as one
who has flourished to be as one seduced to be as one awed to be
as one excluded to be as one who has drifted too far to return

Fragments

pouring gold
into spare, occasional barrels behind their backs
with holes somewhere:

one in the produce aisle, smiling;
one in the cafe, with people and without;
one wanting distantly;
one blind closely;
and one having only so much to give
and waiting till it passes and going on

*

there are dresses in the ether
and here there is nothing—
money spilling across a table
not belonging so much as
evacuating

the value dissolves

*

the dry of rice is a millennium of commerce
the wet of rice is white and abstract

*

you with your fluttering hands raise signals
of dim, trepidatious escaping
bent with the curse of coming always true
to that which always watches

you got a girl pregnant
you made it on as far as Claremont
you with your wife feel time creeping into you here

*

it is gray—all day, all day
the time has come for action and yet stillness sinks like a seed
and spreads outward

Tense

She comes.	She stays.
She is coming.	She is staying.
She came.	She stayed.
She was coming.	She was staying.
She has come.	She has stayed.
She has been coming.	She has been staying.
She had come.	She had stayed.
She had been coming.	She had been staying.
She will come.	She will stay.
She is going to come.	She is going to stay.
She will be coming.	She will be staying.
She will have come.	She will have stayed.
She will have been coming.	She will have been staying.
She would come.	She would stay.
She would be coming.	She would be staying.
She would have come.	She would have stayed.
She would have been coming.	She would have been staying.
She lists.	She goes.
She is listing.	She is going.
She listed.	She went.
She was listing.	She was going.
She has listed.	She has gone.
She has been listing.	She has been going.
She had listed.	She had gone.
She had been listing.	She had been going.
She will list.	She will go.
She is going to list.	She is going to go.
She will be listing.	She will be going.
She will have listed.	She will have gone.
She will have been listing.	She will have been going.
She would list.	She would go.
She would be listing.	She would be going.
She would have listed.	She would have gone.
She would have been listing.	She would have been going.

Secondary Emotions

Horror
Rain: 8-10 inches; winds: 125 mph; storm surge in excess of 15 feet.

Zest
52 degrees Fahrenheit at 10 a.m. and sun; melting snow trickles into the gutters.

Acceptance
Steady rain expected till nightfall.

Astonishment
Sheet metal panels pulled from the roofs of storage buildings, crumpled like paper and dropped in the parking lot. A school bus lodged in the side of a home. The roof of a home in the middle of the road. The remains of a truck wrapped around a power pole. A shovel impaling the trunk of a tree.

Suffering
Record highs of 112 degrees Fahrenheit.

Loathing
Steepening low-midlevel lapse rates with daytime heating and the arrival of a midlevel thermal trough, in combination with modest low-level moisture spreading northward from the gulf, will support the potential for hail with the strongest storms moving east.

Hostility
Northwest winds at 15 to 20 mph likely to bring wind chill readings down to 20 below. Bitterly cold through the night, with a low of minus 10.

Expectancy
A Category 5, 60 miles off the coast.

Fragments

the chill slices time
from August to October
and space from L.A. to
the seas that fan eastward, to
slick planks of wood and
bicycle tires

it is like a hole dug somewhere, looking in,
and the walls are sticky with mucus or
blood, and sharp with thorns or needles

to look into this
to look into the imprint of sisal
a floral print chair

*

this shell of you charred on the inside
with strobe light chemicals and visions,
seventeen away from home,
then thirty-five and here

how—always, again again—each of what it is
each madly different
circumference

*

as strangers become these particular two drinks
then another
the man will look from the table
across the room
and there we will for a moment
and out flicker

*

the cursive letter life of ancestors
the dust of the wings of moths on the skin

*

how to see the world all
through bodies
how everybody tries
everybody

Cerasus

this is born
this thing intact
round

the room, let's see:
a particular dimension
a particular darkness
a particular weight
a particular scent
but the scent is now forgotten

from nothing comes
a seed
a fruit, or perhaps
from some idea

a layer of ending
to wet the soil
then green:
oh miraculous

nothingness draws in taut
at a point
a certain friction of energies—
something

the air compacted
into tiny points of
what? so intense:

poof

Holly Myers

it must have been
the body of a girl then
slender and not thinking
of flesh as anything
particular

a sphere
a globe
a balloon
a thing to be punctured
popped

conviction gathers
the friction of objects
a seed
flesh grows to a point
then grows over and sags

crimson liquid
thin like water
crimson fingerprints
on paper
and from the all of nothing
a child emerges
a mutation of never was
into now

a mark of crimson liquid
proof and
culminations of honor, propriety

the sight of something
unsullied, ungrown
the sheen still

across the skin
like packaging

only three points of memory
properly speaking:
a body in front of a camera
a body in front of a mirror
a body in the darkness, surrounded

a door opened
an avenue cleared
the rubble removed
from the door of a cave

knowledge

as in pie
as in Danish
as in turnover
jam
an organically ordained
intrusion of foreign matter

crimson carpets
rotting
beacons for sparrows

a seed
a tree
a flower
a fruit
a seed

a seed in the belly of a sparrow
a sparrow dead in the grass
near the chair
all afternoon
dissolving over slow time

loss
gain
intrusion
release

a sheet unfurled
out an open window

Tertiary Emotions

Hysteria
Blazing Yellow, 12-0642 TPX.

Jubilation
Viridian Green, 17-5126 TCX.

Tolerance
Eggshell Blue, 14-4809 TPX.

Shock
Methyl Blue, 18-4537 TPX.

Anguish
Haute Red, 19-1758 TCX.

Revulsion
Parfait Pink, 13-2804 TPX.

Rage
Racing Red, 19-1763 TPX.

Curiosity
Beetroot Purple, 18-2143 TCX.

[speculation]

Surface. Surfaces. Shells.

Skin. Eggs. A car. A box. A frosted cake. A book.

Volcanoes.

A stream frozen over.

A hose. A stream of liquid that gels to the air, flows within.

Moss that creeps over the surface of a tree that is rotting out from the inside. A layer of dust. A shell hardens—movement—the shell cracks and pieces scatter.

Maybe it is not surface at all. Maybe it is a gradual hardening throughout. A thickening. From air into mist into liquid into gel into solid. The whole system slows. Piercing the surface. Cutting the skin. Sex. Sharp heat. A blow. A cutting remark. A serious look. Desire. A cold wind.

Fragments

the particular life of this hillside
secures with stone and dry slender brush
what believed itself once to be urgency
your body loses its difference or sweetness
as such
as skin is as the petal of small yellow flowers
as bone is as rock or pellet of hail

*

these songs must be proven somewhere
summertime, and the living is—
summertime—
summertime—

*

it would be coming in circles if only you would
listen
if only from across the city you were to
turn and lay your hand on the head of patience

of course it's difficult

*

there is no path for this
there is noise everywhere

you brighten to the
act of explanation: one of these horses of many
across the plain

Distance

1

Is it running? Is that what you're doing, running?

It's not running.

What is it then?

You have to think of it like—

What? Like what?

Like, think if you are somewhere. Think of it this way. You're somewhere. It's very beautiful. The sun hasn't risen, but almost. There's, like, grass. Flowers. Trees. Dew on the grass. Your jeans are all wet. Say it's the lawn of some big house, and maybe there's been a party. It's nice. But the sun is coming up and you look down the hill and you think: if you start walking now. You know? If you just start walking.

Well? So?

Don't you see what I mean?

No.

When the sun comes up, you'll be there.

Where?

What do you mean? Elsewhere.

2

So you want to walk—is that it? Just walk?

No. Not walk.

Then what are you telling me?

To walk would imply—no. Definitely not. What it would imply, that's not my intention at all.

What would it imply?

To abandon.

Isn't that what you're saying?

No, not at all.

Then what?

To carry and nurture in perpetuity.

At some considerable position of remove.

It is a complicated relationship, near and far. We cannot all love in just the same couple of ways.

What you're describing is not love at all.

You have no understanding of the nature of distance.

PART II
SALOON SONGS

1

Where we sat. Where we were.
Where it came to this and when.
And why and why and why and why
and why.
And why.

Where we sat and where we were
and why.

2

Slipping on the lip
of a martini, slipping on the slice of an orange.
"There were moments of that—
not in a bad way."
Not in a bad way.

What it means now to sit alone,
what it means to sit alone differently.
But I do, I do:
that's not the point.

The sharp moment was—
water to the ankles, forever out,
          not cold.
Melville in the space between distant islands.

3

It was a *fishing* accident you know,
through which the sun glared mercilessly.
It scared the *shit* out of me.

The guy went ta Hahved,
I could tell it from his commas.

Commas, sunk into his speech like thumbtacks.

4

Emotionally I haven't
Emotionally I haven't—
if we start there
because it's drier, to then, the whole Hilton process,
because it's legal,
after which we also talk about alternatives.

> (There is a smell of clams
> and meat.
> Everything he says, he yells, like somehow that will help.
> ding ding applause
> ding ding applause)

These functions, where they drink
and then get serious and talk about buildings
make me think of you
and your helpless, swelling, inevitable bureaucracy.
Your happy hours from 5 to 7
and how you stood in a suit with a drink
and made jokes
and looked away.

5

The skin splits if you exhale
when you exhale
and for that.
This same dream, like before,
he comes.
You're slipping the keys back under his door
and now he cries when he sees you.
You wake up aching. aching. aching.
It poisons you for days.

6

Something to start with—
                        these fissures.
The sun that flares at just that moment
on metal
passing through a doorway.

The fog sharpened into points:
the click of billiard balls,
         here   and there   and there   and again.

7

And then you turned
and away,
at this, the top of this, your hill,
where you were, where you are,
where a wife looks into the face of a child
who was crying
and now sleeps.

8

In terms of—him.
This is what I think, the benefit.
A daughter and a son,
the way I look at it.
She tried to commit suicide two weeks ago.

Oh no. *Oh* no.
Because I know her.
She's 27. I *know* her.
Ironically, she would have wanted to die.

9

How possibly, how *possibly* you come.
You aim and there you are,
                                    that's it.
You aim and there you are.

The china, the movies, the Sunday papers—
the yes, yes, yes, of course:
there is no one dramatic who,
there is no place that's stable.
This turns that and once again.

Let a silence be configured, you read.
You read and wrote it down.

10

How crazy, everything's padded!
Chandeliers, gilt cupids, vinyl!
And everything's forgotten.
It was 1962, or sometime,
when the old German women in black—
when one day once
it just about made sense, or almost.
You have to believe—sometime. Some thing.
[applause applause]

It's named for the magical, mythical lion.
What is ping pong, what is ping pong.
What is Bill diagnosed with Alzheimer's,
when every day became more precious.

And what is the Ming Dynasty?
What, can you tell me, *is* the Ming Dynasty?

11

The envelope of what came
and was lost, and what was lost, the sun.
You distant fucking beautiful thing
with your words
with your words
and your corduroy chair.

12

It was once and
isn't now not but can't—
but can't—
[but, but] but the little silver boat
and what the water means,
                              this inconceivable color,
and this wind, and how it was your childhood
and how now again.

13

Women with cell phones leave the bar
and women with cell phones return.
Imagine.
Where my grandparents lived.
Imagine.
Every day, more evidence.

14

The thickness these male bodies.
The thickness, these toys, these trucks,
these textured voices, these thick, dull eyes,
these bellies in the bar.
Light on black vinyl,
sliding and caressing.
Gentle, amorous, full.

The bellies in the bar, the cool, the bottles on the shelf.

You know the truth is.
The truth is.
The truth is the thick male world
in conversation with itself.

15

You're like   *um*   no.
You're like—enough.
You're sloped shoulders and the death of all,
the bricks falling, paint peeling, from the walls of the cells
around the circle of the blast.

16

Shoulders and shoulders and this geometry;
forearms.
What we're finding beneath clothes
and what we're not.

This
and this
and again:
the radical
stillness
of Wednesday.

17

Of him [his brother] of him
and then,
and through the night, at night, from the desk
across the continent and then the Atlantic.

Of him [his brother] of him
we're thinking.
When for all these second bodies,
for all these things that are not mine
and then.

18

You asked before
and then that's it—
you drift across.
You're looking
                you're looking
        from one
        to another.

We're wandering between the flares.
These things that go
and the quiet
of after.

19

The immensity of the casual we
washes over the afternoon.
What it means
these days   when you go
                when you return.
What it means these days:
your body in a room.

20

You who know
of those of whom
of what this war is waged, the three,
the bedroom voices,
the bed, the wall and then what traces out.
This bed thy center, these walls—
[the three beds]
of each, the three, the voices
                                        the direction,
and these veins of word and blood and otherwise
that trace between the men who talk
to this, thy center,
from where they come
in Denmark.

Are you reading me?
Are you there?

PART III

A Quartet for Explosive Motor, Wind, Heartbeat
and a Landslide

1

There was a bounce in the spring of the seat. Worn red leather. The wide, hard steering wheel and the gearshift long and rattling. *What year'd you say?*

1954.

What? 1954. Voices in the bouncing din and swirl of hot air everywhere; blazing desert noon.

In your family for that long?

Oh no. I picked it up in '85. Rebuilt the engine myself.

2

Land great and flat and tilting. A purple hem around the distant edges, a pine tree shade life somewhere beyond and difficult to imagine in this broad sunlight. Purple smudges, ash green and clay. Billboards hawking moccasins, *authentic.* Arrowheads. *Native American Crafts* and soda.

A howling force across this swell of sandy soil and concrete, visible only by what it moves. There are railroad tracks tracing something more ancient, off there. A train snakes across in ancient time. You watch from the curb of a convenience store. It is possible to imagine horses, manes whipping and churning, up close and at a distance.

3

She. Suitcase open on the floor. She and *her*. Afternoon light round the edges of curtains, a toothbrush. A remote control on the carpet and a plastic cup with water. A shoulder.

4

Yelping voices under the sky, round the east perimeter of a defeated empire, deadened beige block houses. The inversion there, upward, the sky, of what once was vast and impervious to grasping. Children scramble and yell, leading and following, waving sticks and throwing stones. The soles of tennis shoes scrape red mud in streaks across the slope leading down the arroyo.

Four Square

A Love Story

I will say, my love, that I am thinking of sentences with rooms inside. I will say that I have come only to set out swinging again and that it is from this swift and cyclical motion that the crucial patterns of connotation emerge. You will skim across the plains and back at the end of a silken tether. I will leap through fire. I will raise my arms and clouds will splinter into the pages of books and the sun will turn to liquid. You will shoot through the dome of heaven and return with the black of space in your veins, to spill beneath the stones of rivers. At night we will sleep. We will sit with books and glasses of wine and the lights of cities will swell and swoon beneath us.

A War Story

1

He, him, his—out there. Men. Sky. Broad, blind footprints, all overlapping—dust. Men and the scent of bodies moving, and metal, and sun flare glinting, and thick fabric and buckles and belts and bits of plastic and buttonholes. Bodies encased. Bodies lying open in the dust. Dust settling. The ceaseless searing of images.

2

A man bursts into a house full of people. He takes the woman who is his wife. He takes the child who is his son. He tears off down the gravel drive in a white, four-door pick-up truck—dust. On a long frontage road he is intercepted. He opens the door and waves his gun. He shoots himself in the head. The pick-up truck sits for hours, gaping.

A Comedy

A man throws his wife's fur coat out the window and it lands on a woman several stories below. The woman tries to return it. The man refuses. He buys her a hat to replace the one that was crushed by the falling fur coat.

A Tragedy

Show me a hero and I will write you a tragedy.
—F. Scott Fitzgerald

A big room, a crowd, stamping feet and banners. There were a thousand lights. There were balloons. There were policies and procedures mapped across the space, thick and overlapping: operations, security, banquet, housekeeping, signage, sound system, volunteer coordination. Signs were printed in strategic quantities and the mass across the floor was like a great sea, currents of hustle churning through stiller pools of hope and idolatry. Faces were projected twenty feet tall and the crowd laughed and cheered, grasping the nature of its own anonymity, while complex operations wound silent under arms and around shoulder blades. There were men with corkscrew plastic stretching from ear to shirt collar. There were guns and other consequential skills tucked beneath placid surfaces, and many sheaths of weathered papers, held together with clips and in binders. Salvadoran men who'd known their own revolutions stood around doorways in uniforms with trash bags. There were college groups and church groups and faces guarding depths of impassioned conviction and faces bright and blank as plastic.

In a moment, not precisely as scheduled but shortly thereafter, the energy girding all of these movements, these policies and procedures, came into coalescence and all began to swell and churn. Signs waved like grasses across a field; the broad, percussive, aimless noise cohered into a chanting rhythm and all of these streams and currents of life and need and hope and power and demand and baffled, grasping, uneasy desire gathered and flowed in the direction of the stage, to the right of which, behind a curtain, stood a man in a suit with straightened shoulders, tugging on the hems of his sleeves.

Fairy Tales

There once was a woman who gave birth to a stone. It was roughly the size of an ostrich egg, but there was nothing inside—it was solid stone. It was heavy when inside and also when out. It never grew or learned to walk. She kept it on a shelf near her dining room table.

There once was a woman who gave birth to a meteor. It shot straight up from the blood of her loins and tore a hole in the upper atmosphere.

There once was a woman who gave birth to a seed. She did not know what kind of seed it was, or what it needed. She did not know if what she gave it was a planting or a burial.

There once was a woman who gave birth to night. It was very small against the glare of everything around her at the time, the lights and the courtesy and that certain hope. It slipped back over her skin like a blanket and held there for a while and then dissolved.

There once was a woman who gave birth to a fountain. It filled the room and drowned all the doctors.

There once was a woman who gave birth to a force of suction that turned her body inside out. She lay glistening and wet, all her organs bare.

There once was a boy who was born from a pile of twigs. His bones were twigs; he was very fragile. He survived at first on worms and grubs carried in the beaks of thoughtful sparrows, and the language of sparrow was his mother tongue. When he came to crawl and later to walk, he moved with the weightless angularity of a mantis and lived on the fruits and seeds and nuts of the wood and slept in the arm of a willow tree. When he was six years old, he broke his leg leaping from a rocky precipice; thus he learned he was not a sparrow. When he was eight years old, he was taken in by a beekeeper who lived alone. After the language of sparrow, the language of willow, the language of stones, the language of squirrel, and the language of crow, English was his sixth—but then he forgot the others. He learned to read. The beekeeper was a kind and honest man and they worked side by side until the beekeeper grew frail and died. The boy then sold the bees and moved to the city. He became a painter. He never fell in love. He was always very thin. When he was fifty-two years old, he built a cabin for himself on the slope of a mountain, as far as he could get from highways or electrical lines. He learned the language of ponderosa and he was happy there. When he knew he would die, he dug a hole near the foot of the tallest pine, long enough to fit his long, thin body and deep enough to keep him out of the wind, and he lined its floor with boughs and needles. Here he lay in his final days, gazing up at the light through the swaying pines while his pain leached out to the neutral soil. Later the roots of the great old ponderosa grew up in a mesh around his corpse.

A Family Story

I

A stone, one of many.

II

The edge of his skin is the white of these walls.
The edge of his skin is the white of cotton.

He watches the spider on legs of thread, on legs of
slender pencil lines, in the corner, near the book-
shelf. The books are many, they hum and harmo-
nize.

Yes, it will. It does.

Blind motion: flies circle in the heat. A streak of
silver across the road at night.

But that wasn't it—it was something else; he closes his eyes in the glare of the sun. The world is for
a moment the orange of apricot jam.

Again, as he stands at the window. There is
nothing to keep dark from black, he observes.

III

It was not what she would have expected. It was round; it turned against what held it. It glowed from the inside.

He was angry and he held the thing down with his foot. But what is this racket anyway? Who do you think you are?

The thing that she held in her hand—no, she kept her hand closed. But probably it was round. Probably it was red.

In any direction—there is love pinned outward, like a banner. He says, "So you think you will go?" Her hand falls open at the edge of the table.

"You think this road is long," she said. "And you don't even know what's the matter." There was nothing to do but nod.

It was gold, the thing she was holding, and then it rested on her shoulder. It was like a bird. But only for a moment.

"This is how you come?" he said. "With a rain coat?" "I *don't* know," she said.

"No, it is a she." "What?" "No, it is a she."

"The things that are generic," he said, "we look at with our whole selves. That's always how it is. It was just there where you were sitting."

The thing she held was green. It was alive. It was wriggling, but she didn't open her hand.

IV

If this is where you're going with this, then look:
it's mysterious. It is a little thing held. It will come.
But that is not the matter in question.

"You see," she says, "how we are. You see where
these paths lead." "I do but that's not what I came
for." She looks away.

He watched her through the doorway. "Aren't you
coming?" He held his breath. The girl was a streak
of violet across the image.

"So you remember: it's from here, then, into there."
"Is that what she said?" The girl's face was streaked
with dirt. "Are you even listening?"

It was there when they came around the corner,
buzzing with flies. The girl clung to his pant leg.
She didn't cry. He wondered in what corner she
sheltered this clarity.

"It was the sun in those days," she says. "Don't
you remember?" I remember somewhere else,
pine trees. I remember clearings seeped in purple
flowers.

It was green there. It was a flash of green, a piece
of silk. No, not silk—something. It rippled in the
breeze.

"You would think that when it happened—" "Oh,
there was such a commotion!" The wet of wool on
the inside of boots. This thing is an ever shifting
continent.

She looked at him like *of course*: it was in the
way the hem swept the dust. "If you just watch

how they move, how they pull back their hands in wonder." She nearly cried. He reached for the hem, but the girl moved away.

This is not what you'd have thought at first. They came with conviction, they came beating rods in unison. "It wasn't that he disappeared—" "No, it was what became of the animals, something far more delicate."

"Aren't you coming?" "No." The girl on the step, swinging her stick. "Well what are you waiting for?"

It was into this unearthly red, and how the world rippled in the halo of the flames. And how from there he watched the girl on the woodpile. To spend this life unknowing of snakes, he thought.

The sun on the sill where the bones lay. She pointed, knowing already rabbit from coyote. She knelt on the counter in her violet dress. Her calves were golden with dust and her little shoes.

A Ghost Story

I

The thing in the attic, she is a girl in that sense: wobbly knees, holes in places, with skin translucent and blue knotted veins, she crawls like a memory out of a trunk.

In the beginning, with windows and windows and pages scattered and scraps of things, with only sky outside the windows, plain solitude is very broad. Tap tap tap—not knowing her flesh apart from the floorboards. She stitches for syntax a patchwork of echoes:
when—
and, and—
yes—

Though all wrong to the look of her: socks in all the wrong places; bulges and misdecipherings, first nouns without verbs, then only adjectives. Glittering. Godly. Gargantuan. Glib.

Not knowing the sound apart from the wind.

Until one day a tickle—a cough, what—and then: throat, and with it: I. *I* look down and the grounds roll about in green and brown, all color swaying, and voices rise up and the swishing of skirts.

I look up and slip along in the space beneath the bellies of birds.

II

Sequences of revelation, shaky: the skin as mesh or as container? The skin as surface or as mass? The skin with hard bone inside and space stretching from here these small cupped hands to the rafters.

Prepositions clip upon steps, nouns: across, behind, below, toward. Up! Out and down.

There are no thoughts but only investigations. To stand is to cross space; to crawl, to extend a leg. A dip between each floorboard where dust gathers and, in dust, age. A slowing. There are twenty-seven boards from window to window. There are sheets of paper with symbols on them. Time presses in on the sunlight and courses through the wind that moves the green fingers of trees but it slows and lays flat and still across the floorboards.

And between. And regarding. There is *I* between the floor and the ceiling. She lies on the floorboards, looking upward.

III

The grasping is gradual of scale and proximity, when enveloped thus firstly in the breathing of architecture and now it is *there*—beyond—apart from—in front of: the swirl of weather, silver and constant.

It rains and other days the sun shines clear. She doesn't know if she is born or has died or was died or had been born-ing. She sits with the hard round bones of her knees pulled up, knee and knee. A kind of music. Knees with. Knees or. And then *foot*. Her skin but for its few stiff white hairs is soft.

There is a woman whose voice comes threaded with the scent of grass and thus she discovers grass and distance simultaneously.

Or—yes, certainly, below. An or. That she is not.

There are children sounds, and those she is not. There are dog sounds, and those she is not. She makes no sound at all but a low hum in sunlight when the sunlight reaches a certain temperature. The sounds she is not: of curved patches of velvet; of chairs moving; of clocks; of the minute swish of the fibers of carpets; of bread rising; of fingers tapping a marble surface; of the wheels of a toy; of roses fading; of carved wood; of sleep; of coins in a pocket; of coins in a dish; of swallowing; of the slow drying of a closed umbrella; of curtains pulled open and sashes tied; of mice behind cabinets; of steps on stairs; of a wood spoon scraping the bottom of a skillet; of words read from books; of water running; of comfort; of wallpaper coming slowly loose from a wall; of dust settling; of a yellow bird who flutters in through an open door and squeals of delight and exasperation. She comes to see that the house is a thing of rooms. And, and, and, and, and, with walls between. Pockets for the life of animals and things.

IV

She gnaws through the morning on the edge of the windowsill and one day finds that her breath fogs the glass. It grows cold. She pastes sheets of paper to her skin with the rain that drips from a crack in the sill and ties old woolen blankets around her limbs. The words on the sheets she hears in her bones.

I would have written sooner—
How I—
If then—
Promise me—
But—
If only you could see the view from the terrace.

In sentences now, clauses and tenses clicking into joint: She was born. She has died. She lives. She will live. She is long dead by now. Through the winter there is nonetheless a heat welling; she tears pages from books and stuffs them down between the wool and her skin. She dissolves crumbled balls of paper in her mouth. She sees a woman on a terrace, overlooking the sea; there is a pull of some kind. She sees a large bird circling snow covered mountains.

V

She grows in the cold as brittle as paper and moves less over time, though now with the flick of her eye grammar extends. She sees things. There are ships at sea; there are camels in the desert tracing a long slender path in the sand. There are gardens with fountains and blue and white tiles. A man and a woman speak across an ocean in close whisper words like those here in the house—man woman man woman—when the children sleep. If I, then you. My love. I love. *Today I will see Gibraltar.*

She forgets herself. I have long since died and my thought is history pitched forward, places and men. (*I* dwindles.) This is a love letter. This is a novel. A map that is folded and the creases worn. There is a drawing tucked into the pages of a book. She gnaws at books sideways, to poignant clarity. A truth of aloneness stretches—for *I* do not go; *I* do not love—yet overhung by pop-pop-pop, flashing, flashes of light and in the light image and in image place and feeling; her blood is lit with a low gentle flame with sparks. Strange prayers echo over far cities. Men with swords and planes and flashes of red. Marble tables behind a plate glass window with the shadows of letters *B-O-U* and matches, the turn of a lapel against the awning's reflection. A hundred and eight young men on a long colonnade, riotous. An empty bench in a busy station; a cathedral; a room with lattice shutters, light in dusty slender strands. A young woman in a dress. A barge on a river. A little house on a hillside with a gated garden but the house is empty and the day is cold. The boy from the shop was found dead in the wood; his people took him—he was always laughing. A line of soldiers. A line of cots against a burnt orange wall with a high window and hot light and dust floating in with the noise of the street, a jangling noise, with voices and bells. There are twelve ships splintered along the coast line. Bare rocky islands and olive trees; a breeze off the sea; the smell of fish. There is a fish dead lapping against the side of the rock. There are children's fingers refracted in tide pools.

Tell me, Muse, about the man of many turns, who many ways wandered when he had sacked Troy's holy citadel; he saw the cities of many men, and he knew their thought; on the ocean he suffered many pains within his heart, striving for his life and his companions' return.

By springtime she is gorged and motionless.

VI

The floor swings open to the woman with grass in her voice. She gasps. She stands on the floor boards and her head reaches up to the rafters. She opens the windows. With a cloth held to her mouth, she pokes at the pile of wool blankets with a broomstick. Scraps of satin and velvet and white cotton string. Her grandmother's letters, shredded; several old books. She curses. There is a hole eaten out of the side of the trunk.

PART IV

The Aesthetes

Well, if you want to know about that. If that is what you want to know about, well then you should ask them. I don't speak for them, and anyway it's not like I have firsthand information, I only know what they told me. Not that they would lie, because they can't lie, it's against their nature and all their policies, they have a lot of rules. But if you want the full story you should ask them. Of course, you won't be able to find them. Even if you found them, you wouldn't be able to hear them because their frequencies are selective. Maybe if *I* asked them—but you're not going to get me to do that because, frankly, I've had enough of them. Don't tell them I said that. But what it is, they damage things, you see. It is not their intention, they're just too big to get along, though they insist on coming. Their limbs are too big and they break things when they try to move around. Though by limbs you know that I am speaking metaphorically. Their shape is four pronged, as far as I can tell, so, you see: arms and legs or something like them, which is part of why they found us in the first place, but that's another story. So if they damaged me, which they did, and disrupted all that was held up to that point however precariously in balance, I don't hold it against them, not personally, I don't believe it was their intention but merely the awkward, what would you call it, physics. The physiological arrangement. Also because their goal was, in my estimation, virtuous, I am inclined to be forgiving. I am an art historian, as you know. My field is eighteenth-century British landscape painting—or was, in any case. I feel obliged to speak of my work in the past tense, sadly, given the nature of my current predicament, which has drawn me, let's be honest, very far off course. Do you know the painter John Robert Cozens? He has been my primary subject, the focus of my most devoted scholarship, for close to a decade now, and I believe it is due to Cozens that they found me, and this is important, I will try to be very clear: because what they were looking for were points at which—points in the world, I mean, geographical points—at which the concept of beauty, the abstract concept, plugged in, so to speak, to the surface of the earth. Because they can see abstract concepts, which is something I don't think I have explained. They see them as blocks of color, which is difficult for you to imagine, I know. I've had a hard time myself, but that is what they told me. Blocks of color that hover somehow in the space between things, or maybe in another dimension of space that we cannot perceive, though they're not all present at the same time but continually emerging and receding, like, say, windows on a computer screen. That is the best analogy I have come up with. But you should really ask them—I don't understand it. There are many things about them I don't understand, and if you knew what it was like to hear how they talk, their crazed, manic, high-pitched chatter, like bird sounds stretched out and sharpened into edges, no pauses or gaps, no moment to catch your breath. It's terrible. But in any case, that is what they were looking for, those points, and I believe that they identified Cozens as one who possessed some insight in that regard, and if you know his work you will clearly see that they were correct in that, and myself, being the only truly qualified Cozens scholar working today—well, of course they came to me. I suspect they've found others, other vessels, perhaps for other reasons. There are a great many of them, they have a variety of interests. I would not be surprised if you begin to find mathematicians, botanists, linguists, anthropologists who've suffered the same exploitation as I and if I am the only one to speak publicly thus far it is because I am the one who happens to have been put in the unfortunate position of being legally obligated to do so. Which I resent, let me be clear. I've no interest in being a spokesman or an emissary. But with me, and I can of course only speak for myself, what they sought were these linkages, these points of contact, between Platonic beauty and spatial geography. The way it worked, since you asked and I know I passed the question over, is this: I felt them come in, one at a time—I mean successively, not all at once; I counted 37 of them in all, over nearly two years—and I knew this because all my body and especially my limbs began to ache and strain. The strain was such, indeed, that I could hardly move, but I was obliged to move, because that was the whole point, wasn't it, for coming in, so they could feel things and see things and hear things and smell things—because they can't, exactly, in their own form, not as we do—and so then, on the occasion that one of them had taken up residence, we would go outside, we would go places because my apartment, although of course very tidy, is modest in its décor and they wasted no time in telling me it was not a place in which beauty touched down. (My own treasures lie entirely in books, of which I have many, of course, but books don't count for much with them because they can't actually see images that are printed on the pages of books. It is another curious thing about them.) So we'd go out, though to say "we" is misleading for I had no agency in this. That is the thing I want you to understand. I was there but it was as if I was pushed out from the center, pushed up quite flat and thin between them and my own skin if you can imagine that. Imagine, say, that you are in a room in your house so crowded with people that you find yourself pressed up against one wall, unable even to lift an arm while the people on the other side of the room are starting fires and throwing your furniture out the window. That would be a fair analogy. So I was pressed up around the edges like that and I had no choice but to follow them around where they wandered. But what I felt through all that aside from this pressing, which was painful—and this is important, you should write this down—was that my eyes became very, very sharp. My vision. I wear glasses, as you can see. I have astigmatism and I am moderately nearsighted, which means that my vision, when uncorrected, is typically blurry. Like this, when I take off my glasses, it's blurry. Your hair and your face, that window, that plant. But when I was with them my vision was very clear, I didn't need my glasses. And this was interesting but you know I have to say it was also a little exhausting. The clarity was very intense, very sharp edges, almost supernatural. Every surface unbearably bright, every color, as if there were always some other kind of light, I don't know, some brighter light than sunlight streaming in. Things hovered, it seemed. In brightness. As if the brightness was their way of looking, their curiosity, and it held every little thing on all its sides, even behind and below. I did wonder, in moments, whether this was the way that John Robert Cozens saw the world. I don't believe—I have not been able to determine for certain, but I don't believe—that Cozens wore spectacles. And I do believe, though I am not, please note, a religious individual (which makes this whole situation, of course, more

75

than a little absurd). But I do believe that his vision was in-
spired. Whether by God or a pantheistic incarnation of the
spirit of nature, the wind, the four directions, I can't say, but it is
a belief I have quietly sheltered for years, inadmissible, of course,
within a scholarly discourse, but surely—I say it with some hu-
miliation now, because I never intended to leave myself vulner-
able to such apparently mystical operations. I should perhaps
have been more diligent. But surely that is part of the reason
they found me. In any case, whatever they were looking for—I
mean, if it was beauty they were seeking, Platonic or otherwise,
I have to say they squandered the opportunity because here is
what in fact happened: they dragged me all over town, day after
day, sidewalks and stairwells and supermarkets and underpasses
and convenience stores and loading docks, looking only at *ordi-
nary* things, and specifically at things that kept low to the
ground or low to the surface of tables. Tufts of grass at the side
of the road, on the road that leads out along the railroad tracks.
Or the weeds out there, thistle weeds, with little purple flowers.
Or the bits of rust along the, what do you call them, the rails of
the railroad tracks, or the bolts that keep the rails together. The
rails especially. The rails were of great interest. And when I say
that you may presume what concerned them was the engineer-
ing, the structure, or maybe the composition of the metal, but
that clearly wasn't the case because like I said there was a brightness and it held everything, as if everything were in its very self
precious. It was kind of a tender feeling around everything, not
analytic or scientific. And it was visual, it wasn't mental or intel-
lectual. It was a visual feeling. There were no words in it. So
there were the weeds with the purple flowers, there were the
rails. One day it was a little silver cream canister that was catch-
ing the light at a table in the window of a diner, alongside a
metal box that was also glinting. What else? There were count-
less things. One day it was a bowl of oranges. One day it was a
puddle streaked with oil. One day it was the marble on the floor
in the doorway of the old bank building downtown. Of course,
you know about that one. That was the worst of them, I was so
furious, because that day caused so many problems, clearly—all
that business with the security guard and then the police and I
didn't even want to be there in the first place. I did not, I swear

to you. I was stuck in there, all pressed up and helpless and I didn't find the marble at all compelling, even in their glowing way of seeing things, it was just plain, white marble, gray and worn and not even clean, which was what really infuriated me. It was covered in mud from people's boots and dirt because there was snow on the ground outside that was melting. So I tried to move, I tried to leave, I swear I did, but it's not my volition in those moments, I tell you, I could have pushed and pushed for days and it wouldn't have done a bit of good. It was as if in a dream—do you have those dreams? You can't move your legs, no matter what you do—paralyzed. And sometimes people are coming after you, or there are animals. So that was what started this whole business, what brought all these other people into it, like yourself. Oh, I regret that day, I do. Before, they managed to remain discrete, stay out of traffic, follow the basic rules of etiquette, what have you. But now I have all this trouble, all just because of that God damn, excuse my language, dingy block of marble.

Istanbul

One begins with the materials at hand. One begins with the materials that are left behind. One begins—here. And here. And here. A suitcase open on a bed. A new pair of sandals, suede with rubber soles. A floral print blouse; white pleated shorts, size twelve. A pair of pale blue linen pants.

One begins in the middle of other beginnings. One begins long after the crowd has gone and the chairs sit empty and all is still. One begins again as others just go on. It all overlaps. The girl's end began—where? Her beginning ended here, scarcely past the prelude, and all the rest dissolved into silence. Now the chairs are still and bare.

But what was ended is also still present (the woman who is standing here still insists). Still a scent or something like it: a body just around the corner or just at the end of a long distance call. Some call. Some time. Even if it will never come.

And what has begun is tremulous and hollow, driven solely by the insistence of the heart (this heart) to blindly prolong its rhythm and also by the brusque momentum of time. A day passed doggedly, then a week, then two, then a month, then three months, and now so many as fourteen, though the woman resisted it. Fourteen months and twenty-four days and at least a couple of hours. Here, now, it is 11:22 a.m. It is 11:27. 11:52. The end came shortly before dawn. The blinds were still open and she didn't understand how such a thing could happen, how the sky could go gray and the sun could rise.

She begins with a suitcase open on a bed, not willingly. Sandals, linen pants, plastic bags because she read that somewhere. She'd stood in the travel aisle for nearly half an hour—little plastic shampoo containers. (It's just so difficult, Sarah, to even imagine. How can I know? I don't know where to even begin.) The clothes are not enough to fill the suitcase and they are not the right things: a T-shirt with a print like a Navajo blanket, two new packages of socks, canvas walking shoes. There is a silence then around the suitcase, hemmed but not diluted by the clamor in the street of boys from next door, the twins and the younger one with their eternal bicycles and soccer balls. They holler in the summer air, out in an altogether different world. The woman closes the sash of the window.

She is doing this for Sarah. She is doing this *as* Sarah, and Sarah would never have worn such things. Sarah had the face for— well, she was beautiful, and young. She would never have worn canvas shoes or a visor with elastic. The woman has never been young quite as Sarah and no longer would she want to be; the thought, now, of youth comes as a sickening betrayal. There will be *sun* in Turkey. This is a condition of which it is possible to be certain; she will need the visor. Nothing else is certain, though of course there are pictures: ports and temples and caves and ruins and dusty streets and minarets. When she was a child, she had an uncle stationed in Istanbul; he brought her a doll with a brown plastic face.

Day one: Old Christian and Islamic Istanbul. Day two: Istanbul and Ankara. Day three: Ephesus. Day four: Pamukkale. Day five, six, seven, eight, nine, ten. It is difficult to imagine so much time passing. *We must begin to think about moving forward*, said her sister. (She was careful not to say *moving on*.) There will be a bus. There will be thirty other people. They will walk, so she will walk; she's not missed a day of work in months. She goes to work and to church and now she is going to Turkey.

At three, Sarah slipped out the gate at the side of the house and walked four blocks to the car repair. The mechanic found her scrambling among the old tires. At thirteen, she went with the church to Ecuador and lived for six weeks with a family that spoke no English. At eighteen, she went to Mexico. At twenty-one, she went to India. She never did finish college after going to India; she worked at a center there, of some kind. At twenty-three, she met a German and went to Berlin. At twenty-six, she left him and went to Peru. From Peru, she went to Chile, then to Bolivia, and she only ever came home when someone bought her ticket. Sarah once swore she would never die in Minneapolis.

Promise me you'll go to Istanbul. (There was an urgency still, despite the horrific winnowing of flesh. Her forehead gleamed a little in the light of the morning.)

Sarah don't.

When I'm gone.

Sarah.

Promise me.

What would I do in Istanbul?

Live, Mom.

She is a strong willed girl, the woman used to say, not knowing any other way to explain it. Sarah hated this house. For a time it seemed that she *only* hated—the house, the street, the city, her parents. But then something changed and she bloomed like a flower.

There is a hair dryer too, still in its box in the kitchen. She is forgetful anymore. Her sister made a list and taped it up to the refrigerator: *Keep moving. Go to the garden, get your hands in the dirt. Distract yourself (but not with the television).* Later the woman put the list in a drawer. She wrote to her sister but never sent it: *It is better to go to the house of mourning than to go to the house of feasting, for this is the end of all mankind, and the living will lay it to heart.*

She can see Sarah's face and her long brown hair, her long fingers like her father's, picking up the visor and putting it down. Picking up the hairdryer.

Who travels with a hair dryer?

I do.

Mom, you don't need a hair dryer.

I do, Sarah. I'm not like you.

Mom, the hotel will have a hair dryer.

She lowers herself into the chair by the window. When Sarah was nine, she wanted turquoise sneakers; when she got them, she colored over the turquoise with marker. She was lost, in a sense, in Sarah's world. Sarah was never lost. It is possible, yes, the hotel will have a hairdryer, but there are *five* hotels. Sarah? Tell me. There are *five* hotels.

These pieces of the past lay all through the house. There, in the doorway, Sarah is standing. She took Sarah's car keys, she tried to put her foot down, on the advice of a friend who knew nothing about it. (Who else did she have? her husband had gone, he lived in Des Moines with other children.) The girl is red in the face and screaming, just there in the doorway, as if it were yesterday. Her hair was black then and she had a ghoulish look. The mother tried to harden her heart. That night, Sarah climbed out her second floor window and stayed away for nearly a week.

But she came home, didn't she? Home was where she came in the end, and this home, not her father's, and without complaint. She was sentimental, in fact, over little things. The shelf in the tree. The ice cream parlor. An old friend came by in the afternoons and their laughter in the front room seemed to the woman to contain an audible echo of their laughter twenty years before. After all that she had, herself, come to reconcile, the woman would not have expected this: that there was anything in Sarah that would need to return; that there was anything she would have considered lost. Against all the wedding invitations and the snapshots of grandchildren, against the sight of the families that swelled every Easter and stories of children with new homes and careers, she could hold only that her daughter was somehow free, even if it be a treacherous freedom, whose terms ensured her own irrelevance. Only by the time it was almost too late did she realize she took some pride in this.

With the window closed, the room is quiet. The quiet has a thickness; she knows it now as a palpable quality, a gradually incapacitating force, like sleep. Keep moving, she tells herself. A toothbrush, of course—there is no doubt about that. But she moves to stand and she cannot. She's never flown on a plane for so long as that, and she will be alone on that plane, and when she reaches Turkey, she will be alone. She has never crossed the Atlantic Ocean. She has never been to a place where the signs are not in English. For one brief, dark instant, she is furious at Sarah. *I asked for so little; you brought nothing but strife. Now you are gone and still you mock me.* Then the fury dissembles into panic.

Dear Lord, please give me the strength—

But she breaks off with an impatient flutter of the hand. There is a tremor beneath her skin. Her mind is straining to picture life in an unknown hotel but it is like hurling herself again and again down a dark and bottomless well. If there is no hair dryer, if all the signs are in Turkish—she *needs* these things, if Sarah didn't. She is shaking. I can't go, Sarah. I can't, I'm ill. *Mom. Mom, stop.* No—the woman shakes her head in the empty room. Then she shakes her head more resolutely. She does not know if she's refuting Sarah or herself, if she's standing against or giving into the panic. She opens the window; the air is warm and thick and vitally familiar. She has lived in this house for thirty-two years. Whatever happens, she knows where she's at in this house. The window looks down on the lawn with the hedge beyond.

Do you pray Mom?

Of course.

Do you pray for me?

Yes. Many people do.

Sarah was curled in a blanket in a lawn chair. She would never have asked if Sarah prayed. Thirteen months she was home before she died; first she fought, then she didn't. She was angry that she never saw Tibet, or Japan. Then as if by some shift in the substance of the universe, the anger simply fell away. There was no real reconciliation, just a quiet keeping back of questions. It could have been that Sarah found her own God in India, though the woman didn't like to think of it. She found something; she softened; she grew out her hair. The woman wanted to know, but didn't want to ask. Sarah once asked her mother if she was angry at God for taking away her only child. The woman braced by habit against that mean note of irony that often sullied Sarah's pronunciation of *God*, though she wasn't sure, at this moment, if the irony was there or not. *No*, she said.

You believe she's going to a better place.

I recognize that God sees things differently than I.

She hears her daughter's voice more now than she hears God's. It is something she craves but is afraid to ask about. Often her prayers trail off and there is Sarah sitting at the edge of the bed.

Without a hairdryer, her hair will be limp and impossible; she will not look herself, will not *be* herself. These are the things that keep her together: she goes to work and she goes to church and she goes to the supermarket and to the drugstore. There were whole bins at the drugstore of little plastic containers. She stood for half an hour, not knowing anything at all of the world.

She urged Sarah that day to drink up her lemonade and Sarah threw up on the grass; she held the girl's hair and her thin, thin shoulders. Then the girl sank back into the lawn chair and cried.

Those last days were muddled, her eyes were clouded and she wrestled; there was somewhere she was that was not here. She hated the drugs but without them she was reduced so pitifully that no one in the room could stand to watch and she had nothing in her to resist their restoration. Mother and father and step-mother and nurse scrambled for days, adjusting the dosages. This was a torture she would not have expected from God. There is no saying what Sarah thought or saw or felt in the end.

I'm not like you, Sarah. What little I am is here. I am not some old woman on a tour in Turkey.

Why do you keep saying Istanbul? she'd asked at last, exasperated. *Why Istanbul of all places?*

Because you told me once that you wanted to go.

When?

At the lake. You were reading a novel. You told me you'd always wanted to go to Istanbul.

I don't remember that.

I was six years old.

Why do you remember that?

It was the first time I realized there were other places.

Lord give me strength. There is no strength. Sarah was so young; she never wanted heaven. There was a way she had of showing her disdain, but later she learned a kind of patience and it was the most beautiful thing the world had ever seen.

The woman's voice is shaky when she tries to speak. She clears her throat. Her sister's voice is like an arm down from the boat into water. *Margaret, is that you? Margaret is everything ok?*

Sarah here, in her childhood room. Sarah dying, but here. The summer light deepens. Then those boys are there in the street again. A soccer ball slams the door of a garage.

She clears her throat. *Yes, everything's fine. I'm fine.*

You sound faint.

I'm fine. I'm just, well, packing, you know. I wanted to ask you—

Are you ok? Should I come over?

I just wanted to know, well, you see I am packing and I just wanted to know if you think I should bring the hair dryer. My hair dryer. In my suitcase. To Turkey.

Your hair dryer?

Yes.

She is quiet for a moment. *No,* she says gently. *No, I don't think you'll need it. The hotel will have one.*

Is that—common?

Yes, very common.

Ok. That's all. Thank you.

You're alright Margaret?

Yes.

I'll be by at six, ok? To pick you up.

Yes.

You're going to have a good time Margaret.

Ok, well, good bye then.

The toothbrush, keep moving. The walking shoes, the visor. She is going to Istanbul, she must, in the morning.

The Guest Room

Her first night in the house in San Luis Obispo she became aware of the breath of the previous owners filming all the floors and walls. It was thin and clear, like Vaseline; it pulsed slightly. She bought three gallons of bleach and spent the next four days scrubbing, beginning in the bedroom and working outward. Sounds arose as she wore through the layers, faint and rippled, like the murmur of a restaurant heard from a distance. She plugged her ears with bits of toilet paper and tried to inhale as little as possible. She changed the water every six square feet.

Aiden's mother assured her she would love San Luis Obispo. A college town. Lots of young people. The house was a 1924 Craftsman bungalow with dark wood floors, a stone fireplace, stained glass in the dining room, a narrow kitchen with a door to the back, one bathroom, two bedrooms, a linen closet. It was presented to her as a graduation gift, but came tangled in the same obscure legal netting that everything she had came tangled in—her father's signature on every page—and that left her always a little unsure of just how it was she could be said to exist. A good investment, he said, a good time to be buying, a charming little place, a steal.

The furniture came from the Palm Springs house, which her mother had lately determined to redecorate. The bed was wide and heavy and took up most of the room, with a carved oak headboard and a comforter covered with roses. When she grew weary of scrubbing, or the noise grew too loud, or she began to feel the residue of breath sticking to the skin of her arms or her face, she showered and changed and lay on the bed to read. Reading calmed everything. She lay and her body took on a different meaning, her thick flesh no longer an obstruction but a conduit, through which rippled the sensations of other heroines. She'd come to this house with five new books, two Joan Conways and three Caroline Lanaways, stowed at the bottom of the suitcase that held her winter sweaters, where her mother wasn't likely to find them. She stacked them on the nightstand in the order she intended to read them, with her inlaid butterfly box on top. The Conways were modern but the Lanaways were history and she wanted to begin with the Lanaways.

When in her scrubbing she reached the front door—the outer reach of her expanding circle—she stepped outside, it was June. There were houses across and to either side and the proximity was vaguely confusing. There was a man in the driveway of the house to her right, loading boxes into the back of a truck. He wore shorts and a baseball cap and looked like a man from a movie about something that happens in a neighborhood.

"You must be our new neighbor," he called, coming to the fence with one of his boxes. "I'm Chris Johanson. My wife is Carrie, and we've got a little one, Tyson." He was slender and athletic and he moved with lightness, as if eager to be running or climbing mountains. He paused and grinned and she knew she should say something. "Is it just you in there?" he asked.

She nodded.

"Where did you move from?"

It took her a moment. She was aware of a moisture beneath her breasts. "Santa Barbara," she said.

"My wife is from Santa Barbara. Originally. We moved here from Portland. She teaches at the university."

Aiden nodded again.

"Well, I better get on. You let us know if you need anything."

On the fifth day she unpacked the boxes in the kitchen, then the boxes in the bathroom. Then she went to the grocery store. On the sixth day she lay in the bedroom and read, drinking apple juice and eating saltines. The first book concerned a Civil War nurse who fell in love with a Union soldier. It was a dreary setting in Aiden's view, and she felt a little sick at the thought of blood mixed with mud, which was something the author dwelt upon repeatedly. The second book took place in Scotland. The heroine was the daughter of a feudal lord whose brother was killed in a war with the British. Though promised in marriage to a neighboring duke, she fell in love with the captain of her brother's regiment, who was a scoundrel in love but hero to the cause of Scottish liberty. When Aiden closed her eyes she saw him crashing through the door of a dark, low-ceilinged room with an enormous fireplace, while the heroine—or someone, some woman—sat washing her feet in a tub of water, her night dress slipping low across her shoulder.

On the evening of the sixth day, the ants appeared. There were three of them, black and tiny, across the counter beside the kitchen sink. She smashed them each with a paper towel and dropped the towel into the trash. She found two more circling near the coffeemaker. The sight of them confused her: had the bleach been insufficient? She dispatched with the two and went on with her evening.

The next morning when she woke there were ten times as many, moving in a trail down the wall from the edge of the cabinet and up the side of her apple juice glass. It frightened her. She rinsed the glass, dropping it once when an ant made it onto her hand, then smashed the others with a paper towel in their long configuration. She waited for more from the gap beneath the cabinet but the march appeared, for now, to have ceased. She took out the bleach and scrubbed the counter again, then set about rushing to get herself together.

It was her first day of work. She made coffee and sat at the dining room table with the two cherry Danishes she'd bought herself special, in her new lime green skirt and matching blazer. She was to be an accountant, like her father; she had a position at a firm several blocks away, run by one of his former employees. She told herself it was a bright new start, that in this new real world she would live among adults, not juveniles. She told herself she would be a success.

That evening she found another trail, on the other side of the sink, onto the plate with the crumbs from the Danishes. There were more of them this time. She smashed them with a handful of paper towels and tried to wipe the line toward the sink, knocking the plate such that it clattered and broke against the walls of the basin. There were so many; they scrambled out from under the paper towels and up the walls of the sink; they scrambled onto her hands and her wrists. She saw now in their encroaching multitude that they were not themselves individual agents but rather the few yet visible particles in a giant creeping wave. With each tiny, tickling touch she felt a dark haze creeping up her arms. She cursed as she shook them off, then pulled out the sprayer and flooded the counter, using wads of paper towels to steer them toward the sink. They curled into balls when the water hit them, like a hundred free floating decimal points gliding about the floor of the sink. When they were all washed away, she waited for more but, again, the march appeared to have ceased. She pulled the bleach from beneath the sink and scrubbed the area once again.

She'd bought herself a frozen lasagna special, along with two candles to go on the dining room table, but she couldn't bear to pull it out of the freezer, with the kitchen contaminated now as it was. She had her dinner at a nearby sandwich shop, watching a man through the window who was pacing the parking lot, yelling obscenities into a cell phone. On the way home she bought two bottles of ant spray.

The next day there were no ants, neither morning or evening. In the evening, she baked her lasagna and ate it cross legged on the bed while watching a program about Queen Elizabeth. She began the third book curled up in the bath, her body ballooned in the water about her. This one was set in the American Revolution. The heroine, an orphan, was raised by a wealthy Massachusetts landowner but cast out when he died by his jealous son and forced to work as a servant for the leader of a local regiment.

On Thursday morning, Aiden opened the cabinet to find the ants swarming a box of breakfast cereal. Two days later it was the sugar dish she used for her coffee, then a bag of oatmeal cookies, then an empty can of diet soda, then the trash can. The bustling spectacle filled her with revulsion; she sprayed each object of the creatures' devouring, sprayed the long, awful, wriggling trail, sprayed everything around, all cracks and crevices, then watched the ants curl and writhe in the poison. Once, in a fury, she sprayed everything in the cabinet—cereal, coffee, potato chips, spaghetti, ramen noodles, cans of soup—and had to throw nearly everything out.

Having erased the stain of her human predecessors, Aiden was thus now certain of another intelligence, dark and inhuman, welling in the cabinets, the walls, the earth beneath the house. When she stood in the kitchen, she felt its motion beneath the stillness. Its blind determination appalled her. It sent its scouts, it sent its troops, it tried one angle, then another, and she met each assault with a proprietary sense of injustice—the food was *hers* and the house was *hers*. But there was a hemming futility: it did not see her. She meant little more to its tactical perception than a heavy rain storm or a tractor tire. It comprehended her existence from an ancient and amoral reservoir of consciousness, from which perspective her life, the lives of her predecessors, and the life of the house, for all its mass, all its charm, were merely temporary intrusions. She stood her ground, then, yes—but what did she stand on? She defended—but what did she defend? It was like standing alone in a very dark room.

After a while, the onslaught subsided, with she the apparent victor, having poisoned every inch of the kitchen and moved all that was permeable and perishable into the safe house of the refrigerator. Time went on. In the absence of the ants, her life had a bland rhythm. She left for work at a quarter to nine. On Saturday she cleaned, on Sunday she rested. Her mother called every evening at seven. She finished the American Revolution. When she imagined the hero, she saw Chris Johanson—only now a widower, his wife raped and killed by British forces, his little son drowned in a raging river. When she closed her eyes she saw him bounding up a hillside, crashing through the doors of a barn, where she—the heroine—wavered on the brink of the very fate that befell his wife. She—the heroine, with her slender arms and narrow waist and breasts neat and modest and milky white—lay where she'd been thrown in the hay, her skirt hiked up above her knees. She—Aiden—read through the evenings, in the bath or the bed, and when she finished the book, she read it again.

One Saturday morning when the sky was overcast, Carrie Johanson appeared on her doorstep with the child and a purple tin of cookies. She apologized for taking so long to stop by, said she'd been up to her ears in papers and exams and they were leaving the very next day for Wisconsin but she wanted to leave these cookies as a housewarming gift. She had a capable air beneath the weight of her child and smiled at Aiden with alarming sincerity.

"You're getting along ok? Such a charming little place." She bounced the child and looked around. "Dan and Jeremy were sick to sell it. They were wonderful people, but this economy, you know. They had a restaurant in town but it went under. Anyway. Chris said you're all alone over here. Is that true? You look so young. Well, we'll be gone for three weeks, but after that—come by anytime, come by for dinner, we'd love to have you."

The window in the bedroom looked out to a hillside behind the house and Aiden lay with the tin of cookies, trying to discern the ants' dark essence spidering through the soil. They were somewhere, surely; they remained. They were everywhere but here. She looked at the hillside and imagined their trails weaving just above and below the surface of the soil, weaving a thin black lace that quivered as it lay, covering everything.

It was quiet with the Johansons gone. A girl came every couple of days to water the plants in the front and back yards; sometimes she went in and played music in the house. Hard music, with guitars. There was a boy with her once and they stayed inside with the music on for nearly four hours, in some invisible reach of the house, beyond the sight of the windows.

On a Saturday night, the ants returned. There were four cookies left—she'd been saving them for Sunday—but she'd forgotten to return the tin to the refrigerator; by morning it was subsumed. She stood for a moment, shocked. She didn't know how she could have made such a slip, how she could have grown so complacent. She watched them in their slithering lines, blind in their triumph, smug and silent, and perceived in a flash and with fearful clarity the immensity of all that surrounded the house—soil, sky, city, continent—and the legions of forces she had to contend with, all driving ever at her and intertwining, though the things that she wanted were so few and simple. She wept as she drowned them: the ants, the cookies, the careful layers of yellow tissue paper. She wept as she sprayed, wept as she scrubbed, muttering and cursing. She wept as she folded herself into the bathtub, pulling her bathrobe over her head, and when the weeping ceased, lay still there, bent and cramped in the quiet, through the afternoon.

The next day—Monday—she called in sick, and then again the next. On Wednesday she rose, dressed, had her breakfast and paused as she struggled with a buckle on her shoe just outside of the door to the guest room. There was a hush about the room, with its matching bamboo furniture so familiar to her from the guest room—her room—in the Palm Springs house. There were palm trees on the bedspread and matching lamps in the shape of giraffes, one on the dresser, one beside the bed. She adjusted the buckle and stood. There was a terrible vacancy. She went to the kitchen and took the sugar dish from the refrigerator, then returned and deposited a small pile of sugar onto the rug beside the bed. She watched it for a moment. Then she left for work.

That evening, there was a single trail, slender and tentative, leading from somewhere beneath the bed. She brought the sugar dish and made three more piles, one in each corner save that with the door. When she went to bed, there were a handful of scouts; by the time she woke the following morning, there were trails consuming all three piles. She lay down another half dozen piles, one foot in from the molding and two feet from one another. She sprayed a line of poison across the doorway, then shut the door and went to work. That evening, she lay down another ring, one foot in, under the furniture when necessary. Then she lay on her belly on the bed and watched the trails, weaving and rippling across the floor. She wondered if there was a central intelligence—an office somewhere, a cavern where the decisions were made. She wondered if the ants had feelings. Over the next two days, she lay down several more circles, working toward the center, bending precariously around the edge of the mattress to spoon out piles under the bed. Then she lay back on the bed and imagined herself in a stone-walled room, high in a castle besieged by rebels. The sounds of battle thundered: cannon fire, rifles, the clanking of swords, the cries of men in fury and dying. There was a maidservant with her, clutching her waist and whimpering in terror. Footsteps thudded through the corridor, then shoulders pounded and splintered the door around its lock. There were five men; they approached in silence and surrounded the bed. They were bloodied and filthy and rank with sweat. The tallest nodded to one of the others and that one tore the girl from her arms, wailing and kicking, and carried her out. She vowed as the others approached not to scream or make a sound, fierce in the dignity of her birthright. They cut her gown from her body with daggers and took her from above and from behind, one by one, pinning her arms and holding her hair in their fists.

Through all the next morning she sat on the bed, watching the trails grow thicker and darker, like a network of tributaries swelling in the spring. There was a kind of peace in being thus suspended with this darkness roiling ceaseless beneath her, consumed in the logic of its own motion and blind to the looming treacheries of scale. They are strategic, she thought, but clearly not wise. She wondered which was more important in the end.

On Sunday, she filled the sugar bowl again and set about laying a smaller grid—half inch piles, two inches apart—across the surface of all the furniture: dresser, table, chair, bed. She did the bed last, careful to step between the trails. Then she closed the door, sprayed the threshold again, and left it closed for a week.

Her mother called every night at seven; Aiden told her that she was happy in the house; that her coworkers liked her; that she was beginning to find her way around town. The Johansons returned, waving and smiling as they unpacked their car. She went to work every morning and came home every night, changed into sweat pants, sometimes drew a bath, and had her dinner on the bed in front of the television. She bought three more Lanaways—a Regency, a Victorian, and another American Revolution—and finished all three in the course of that week, reading late into the night.

On Sunday morning she dressed and had her coffee on the back porch with a chocolate croissant. It was August now; the sun was hot and the greenery up the hillside had a dull, golden glow. She wondered if there were snakes up there. Chris Johanson and his son were romping about the lawn next door, the father groaning like a swamp creature, the son squealing and scampering. She washed her dishes and set them to dry, then put on her tennis shoes and a pair of gardening gloves and tied a dishtowel around her nose and mouth. She stood at the door for several moments before opening it, telling herself she would need to work fast. There would be chaos, confusion. She imagined the darkness churning up like clouds of dust around a scuffle.

There were ants everywhere—thousands, millions. A twelve-by-twelve foot weave of blackness over floor, bed, dresser, chair. She began at the doorframe and worked methodically in long strokes, from one end to the other and back again, laying the poison like primer across the floor and all the furniture and up the lower reaches of the wall. It glistened in the light. The ants scurried around the edge of each stroke, but when the poison came upon them they slowed and curled and twitched and went still. A million decimal points, carpeting the room; life returned to a state of abstraction; one writhing branch of a massive strategy foiled.

When at last she'd covered every square foot of the room, she stopped and looked around. The bedspread was damp; the dresser glistened, and the stiff wooden flesh of the giraffe lamp.

There was a streak of moisture across the cream colored shade. She considered opening the window but didn't. She left the two empty cans on the floor near the dresser. At the door she paused and unlaced her shoes, leaving them just inside the threshold. She removed her gloves, then the dishtowel, and draped them over the shoes, then her socks and her sweat pants and her t-shirt and her underwear. She stuffed a folded bath towel into the crack below the door, then stood in the hall in her copious skin, the victor, alone.

A Cylindrical Object on Fire in the Dark

A boy lay in the street. A young man, maybe twenty. Nobody
came. She watched from her window for more than an hour;
later he was gone, but he left a shoe and a scrap of yellow cloth.
She didn't know how to behave in a war. She locked her windows and taped over all the outlets in the kitchen, which seemed
to help a little.

The noise through the war was intermittent but immense. Ex-
plosions set car alarms squawking down the block; guns rattled
in the night and men hollered orders down alleyways in unfamiliar languages. One day a bomb went off in the café by the
square and trucks droned and lurched for nearly a week, push-
ing enormous blocks of concrete into piles. Children wailed
in adjacent apartments and as the war went on the walls grew
thinner. The bigger noises had a physical force; the walls of the
building shook the boxed up air like a sifter and what came free
settled soft, a kind of soot, across the carpet. She had one pair of
boots—she couldn't remember who left them. They were men's
boots. She wore them every time she walked across the carpet,
but the stuff that fell from the air seeped in through the eyelets.

She came to suspect that memories shook loose with the plaster,
for with each passing day she found herself with less to go by—
faces were strange and connections eluded her—until it seemed
that the war had gone on forever, that there had been nothing
in her life beyond the war, and that she'd never known another
person. One must sacrifice, in a war, to future generations. She
left clothing in parcels on the step of her building; by morning
the parcels were always gone.

She was not especially afraid but she was often confused. She
wandered the streets in the daylight hours, keeping within a
four or five block radius; she sat near a tree in the square and
watched the trucks. An old woman gave her bread and called
her by a name she didn't recognize, though food was not, as it
happened, what she was short of just then. The woman showed
her a photograph and wept. When she left the woman's apart-

ment, the streets were wet with dirty rain and night was still a long way off. Without memories, her days were spacious but long; she grew bored. She knew there were parts of herself she was squandering.

She found a handful of bills in a dresser drawer. The timing was fortuitous for she had very little to wear: a nightgown, a coat, a few mismatched socks, and something that looked like a bridesmaid's dress with a scalloped bodice of pale green satin. Of what she'd had, these things were all that remained because these were all she was able to manage. There was something about denim that made her choke; the blue jeans in the bureau she'd discarded long ago. Undergarments, too, threw her into a panic—the imprint of elastic in tender places. There was a shelf in her apartment of medical textbooks and she had read a great deal about the circulatory system; she knew that blood carried oxygen from the lungs to the brain and carbon dioxide from the limbs to the lungs and any constriction of this process made her light headed and ill. She felt that she needed her full faculties about her.

But there was a department store a few blocks down that sold dresses and housewares and linens at discount; with what she had she guessed she could pay for seven dresses, which struck her as a very satisfying number. She decided to acquire them at regular intervals, so as to avoid arousing suspicion, and was relieved at last to have found a vocation.

The parameters, however, were far from evident; she made several fruitless trips at the start. The patterns, the colors were too garish or too plain. The music piped in had a scraping quality and she was uneasy beneath the gaze of the clerks, who were younger and made of some harder substance. She soon began to doubt the merits of her enterprise.

Then one morning she saw a peculiar thing: in the charred remains of the café by the square, on a stretch of linoleum blackened by truck tires, lay a piece of a mirror roughly the size of her hand that held as if in a bowl the blue of the sky. It was so startling an inversion that she stood frozen for a time, trying to work out just what she was seeing—a blue so perfectly clear and pristine that it belied the veracity of all that surrounded it, even that of the sky itself, which overhead was pale and scattered with clouds. A man yelled down at her from the seat of a bulldozer. She bent to retrieve the mirror, to take it home, but the blue slipped off and disappeared. Carefully, then, she let it lie, pulling a chair in front to protect it from the bulldozer. The following day, to her wonder and amazement, she came across just the same shade of blue in a short sleeved, knee-length, belted waist sun dress lodged in a rack of dark-colored blazers and she understood the nature of her obligation. When she pulled the dress from its bag in her bedroom, a purer, truer sky was revealed. When she wore it, she knew she had become invulnerable.

She was to be, then, a link, a kind of conduit. There were magnanimous forces smothered by smoke; it fell to her to endeavor to keep these lines open. Every day for a week she wore the blue dress and there was a calmness around her, the noise held off. There was a haze in the air but it didn't penetrate; she shone. There was no pride in this, it was a humble, hollow feeling.

She began to watch for salient colors and noted each when she found it in the margins of a book, using the most descriptive language possible. Later, she looked for each color in the store. One day, it was the silver-white reflection of the dawn on a triangular shard of glass in a window. *Like a wedding dress covered in sequins and beads*, she wrote. But this was not quite right. She added: *No not the color of the fabric but the color of the reflection of the fabric in the beads.* (She looked for days for this one but found no match, which dismayed but didn't entirely discourage her. She knew, of course, that the path would be long.) The skimming red flash of the lights of a fire truck against a whitewashed wall after midnight. *Like a hard cherry candy taken out of one's mouth beneath a street light.* (She came closer with this one, spotting a red vinyl belt, but a belt wouldn't do—she was again unsuccessful.) The green lining of a coat belonging to a man who sat on a curb with a blood-soaked cloth to his head. The coat was torn and gaped at one side. Other men stood around the curb, speaking words that had shape but no meaning, gesticulating urgently. *Like grass in a shadow in a photograph with sunshine.* The next day she found a grass green party dress. It was short and tight—it didn't suit her but that was not a concern, she wore the dress for its sake, not hers.

It was not until dress number four or five that she began to work out the details of the project in earnest. She did so across the back pages of her book: 1. The colors are portals, transitional spaces, linking our own world of chaos to another beyond where the air is clear and things exist without shapes. 2. Everything in this world has its origin in that, just as all the pictures in a book have their origin in ink. 3. *All* colors mark the thinning of a membrane. *These* colors mark a fissure or tear and the brief emergence of the purer thing. Ex.: Sky-ness (a simple one). Grassshadowphotograph-ness. 4. It is a direct and fundamentally mechanical phenomenon; there is nothing divine or celestial about it. 4a. There is no such thing as God. 5. That said, the implications are profound. We preside in a purgatory where nothing is whole, where cigarette butts are left to gather in the gutters and dead men's shoes are abandoned to the rain. Color is an echo of the real world beyond.

Her body, she felt, had became a beacon. She was filled with compassion for the suffering of others and when she looked around now she saw this suffering everywhere. Food was scarce and electricity uncertain. Bombs dropped from planes that flew with no pilot. The sky, once inert, assumed a sinister aspect, and two blocks down an entire family was killed, two women and four children and a disabled uncle, without warning in the early morning hours. She stood in the crowd in her grassshadowphotograph dress as the body of a child was brought from the rubble and given to the arms of his surviving father, who took him but faltered as perhaps he fainted and those standing by rushed in to catch them both. She didn't know what the green really brought to this circumstance. The boy wore a purple t-shirt and one brown sock, but these were bloodied and stained and the colors smothered. She remained, however, and did what she could.

It was around this time that the war made it into her apartment. The hallway was dim, he forced his way in, and once inside he drew all the curtains. He was heavy of step and wore a thick, dark beard and he spoke to her but she didn't understand, then he set about sending messages to comrades using the blue gas flame of the stove. She hadn't noticed before that this was possible: that the burners turned the air to shimmering glass and that this glass could be used as a screen for projection. He tried to force her to do it for him, pulling her roughly toward the stove, but she screamed until he let her go. She watched him then from behind the table but wasn't able to decipher the code.

He ate a great deal. And he slept with a machine gun curled up in his arm. At first, he slept upright in an old beige arm chair whose back he pulled up against the front door. He seemed to have a great debt of sleep; it weighed on him and sunk him soon into other chairs and at last into a large, dark pile on the bed, where he slept without moving for nearly twelve hours. She watched him, trying to understand. His trousers were brown and his boots were black and his jacket was a very dark shade of green, one that may indeed have been green in word only—he had, in fact, no real color at all and as he lay there on his stomach with his face to one side she came to believe him to be not a positive entity but something more like a pit or a hole. She watched from just outside of the room, afraid of the gravity he might still exert. It would be, that gravity, like an undertow.

She pored over her textbooks but found no explanation. Blood fluid, she learned, is made up largely of plasma and that plasma is ninety-two percent water by volume. It is straw yellow in color; it circulates nutrients. But what is color in the dark of the body? Or yellow dissolved in a greedy red? Later she donned her blue dress and ventured closer. There was a smudge on the hand that lay over the gun: grease or ink or some burn of the iron life of the gun (which was not life, of course, but the opposite). She knew that blood turns bright red when its hemoglobin is oxygenated, dark red when it is deoxygenated. There was a dark red smudge on one of his sleeves. She touched it, even; it was stiff and matted. His being is a vacuum, she thought; there is no air in his clothes. He did have a gravity, but the force was weak.

She came, as he slept, to a more nuanced conception of death. She worked it out on a scrap of paper torn from an empty bag of flour. 1. Death is not an occurrence but a substance, a toxin present in degrees. 2. It is highly concentrated in acts of violence, though can be passed in a myriad of gentler ways. 3. It remains in the flesh of any butchered animal. One is exposed, therefore, from an early age. It builds in the bloodstream, circling constantly. 4. It passes into sewers and onto the streets and anywhere else men bleed or urinate. 5. Fruits and vegetables are highly susceptible. She paused here, then added: (Exceptions? Apples, oranges, grapefruits, lemons, kumquats, avocados, coconuts, olives.) She resolved to abstain from meat and poultry and any vegetable that grew near the ground.

When he woke, she was crouching several feet from the bed, trying to determine from a safe enough distance whether there was light behind the lids of his eyes. His eyes were like coal, even when open. He jerked when he saw her and grasped at his gun, and there was a little light yet: it flickered for a moment there in the confusion. But once he'd regained himself it flickered out. He pointed his gun at her and began to yell. She wanted nothing to do with his language. She wasn't sure there was anything in him worth saving.

They argued in the kitchen. He gestured toward the empty cupboard, then toward his own mouth, then toward the door. Yes, he is a pit, she thought, sloshing with death water. She wanted to tell him he had no need for food but he'd found her money and wouldn't hear of it; he put the bills in her hands and shoved her toward the door. He took his gun and pointed it at three framed photographs that stood on the shelf not far from the door, but the people in those photographs were strangers to her. She shrugged. He shoved her again and she was out the door.

She tried to see through the chaos to the shapeless world, the world that was real, where red was just red, but found that the portals were getting smaller. She walked for hours and perhaps he watched her, for he was often watching the street through the curtains. She told herself she couldn't help that. The old woman took her in and gave her a bowl of thin, salty soup. She said to the woman: How strange this place is, with all the bombs and broken paving stones. There was a ceramic vase on a windowsill there with a yellow glaze that caught the light. *A yellow satin dress on a brown haired doll,* she wrote in her mind (for she had no book). No, that couldn't be right. *Autumn leaves overhead, in cool bright sunlight.*

That very day she found the matching dress, though she told herself: this is a funeral color. She was uneasy in a way she could not articulate. But there it was in the very front of the store, autumnleavescoolsunlight, with a ruffle at the front. This was number six. She paid the cashier and changed in a corner, rolling her green dress into a ball and putting the last of her money into her boot where the coins dug into her still soft sole.

Dusk had fallen by the time she returned. The soldier, finding her empty handed, threw her against the wall in the kitchen. Clearly, she could see, the water had risen. He beat her in the face until her left eye swelled shut; she slid to the floor and he kicked her in the stomach. The hemoglobin was oxygenated, it spread in vivid red blotches across the patterned linoleum. Then he left the room and perhaps she slept. It was dark. She didn't move—she told herself: a funeral color. Yellow satin on a brown haired doll in the morning. Somewhere, she thought. That was somewhere particular. A yellow satin dress and little black shoes and pale legs. Then she heard the door to the apartment close and a dead yellow light flooded the kitchen.

He pulled her up by her arm and pressed a carton of rolled oats to her chest. His grip dented the carton and the lid fell off and he shoved it again against her chest and she coughed. Up very close the man smelled of metal and sweat and some unfamiliar kind of soil. She made oatmeal, then. She didn't care anymore.

He sat nearby with his gun on his knee and soon enough he began to talk, first in muttered or barking tones, later more congenially. He was telling her something of his pointless life. After he ate, he showered for a very long time and she lay down again at the spot where the blood had dried.

He stayed for three more days. He wanted in some appalling way to love her. He disappeared occasionally for short intervals and returned with food in one form or another and meanwhile the building had gone very quiet. Children no longer wailed through the walls; footsteps were infrequent. Bombs fell still from time to time, but none near enough to shake the walls. It was as if the war had narrowed in on her absolutely, at least insofar as her building was concerned. It was she and the war in this small apartment; all that she did now carried a heavy consequence. But what could she do? There was no seeing into him. He was a lightless being, charred through.

He tried to wash the blood off her dress but she screamed when he touched her so he let go. He stood back and motioned up with his arms. She'd thought at first that he must be a hundred years old but he'd shed several decades in the shower, it seemed, and now he might as well have been a boy beneath the crusts of his beard and his clothes. Once he smiled and the smile was a knot in the light. Again, he motioned up with his arms. It is a funeral dress, she wanted to tell him. She wanted him to know that he was not real, that there was a truth beyond him that he would not reach so long as he cleaved to the realm of metal and smoke—but the yellow dress was not the right path. He persisted, however. She took off the dress. He stood staring and his eyes were like hungry stones.

Should she fight him? Is that what this called for? Should she submit and be fought, as she had in the kitchen? What did one do in close quarters with a war—was it better to rile or to attempt to pacify? So long as he was here and well fed, he would not be out dropping bombs on children. She had no children and she was no longer herself; and she had the time, she had no other plans. Should she soothe him and calm him? Should she get hold of his gun? If she subdued him, would the war come to an end?

She could do nothing standing naked in her boots on the tile. She was no beacon here, her skin was opaque. He gave the dress back to her, dripping, but she didn't move, so he pulled it over her head and reached up underneath to push her arms through the holes. This took some time for she offered no help, unable to move in his tangled field. The blood stains had turned a dull pinkish brown, which seemed to her a very bad sign.

He left and returned with three bags of flour. Then he left for a longer time and returned with two eggs. He was very pleased. He stood in the kitchen and seemed to be explaining something, his machine gun slung across his back. He moved around her from cupboard to cupboard; what he made in the end was a kind of pancake. She wasn't certain about eggs, since they were related to poultry; they were not butchered, of course, but birthed, which was the opposite, but then cracked on the edge of the bowl by a soldier—was that violence? A shell with the shapeless thing inside, with a color—yellow—suspended in space. (Yellow but a richer hue, with orange, thicker than the light through autumn leaves.) She tried to get up to fetch her notes on death but he pushed her firmly back down in the chair. His touch had become distressingly familiar. He wanted her to eat but she wouldn't eat and he hit her so hard on the back of her head that her face nearly went into the pancake. He sat beside her and placed the fork in her hand.

Was this what the war had come down to then—two willful people alone in a room? Grieving suddenly for the loss of that more perfect yellow, that sun-like sphere inside each of those eggs and indeed inside all the eggs that ever were, she began to cry. She ate half the pancake and that seemed to appease him; he ate the rest and four more besides.

While he watched out the window through the narrow slit curtains, she tried to sort out her thoughts in the margins of a text book. 1. —she wasn't sure where to begin. She was born somewhere, surely. But that was not relevant. She tried then again to take stock of what she'd learned. That it is the hemoglobin that carries the oxygen. That hemoglobin is a protein molecule. In fact, it is four proteins: a quaternary structure, four globulin chains arranged in sets of alpha-helix segments connected in a fold arrangement. Was that right? It was difficult, her thoughts were like fluttering moths. But she felt a kinship with hemoglobin, a commonality, roaming the streets as she did in green and blue. Perhaps the colors were proteins? No, they were more like oxygen. No, it is oxygen that activates the color: bright red across the floor; the blue of the sky. She wasn't sure. She had one dress to go but here she was trapped, and she was growing tired.

1. (She tried again:) War is exhausting. 2. Yes—because it constricts and it smothers. The door is blocked by an old beige armchair, while outside there are children being crushed under roof beams. Without oxygen, the system gradually weakens. 3. Is there anything one can do to resolve it, or 4. Will it go on like this until the end of time?

He kept his machine gun always on his back; there would be no getting it away from him. If she killed him, would everything go back to normal? She no longer knew what normal was. Could she stab him, could she cut his throat? Did she have the strength to strangle him? Yes, she thought, she might have the strength. But if she killed him then she would never be rid of him, which was the problem with the logic of the war in the first place. It was a vortex of need, it fed on itself. Once butchered, a body spills death all around.

He seemed bewildered, at the window, by the inactivity. He would look down to the street, then up at the sky. He paced. The electricity went out and he sat in the dark, very still, with his elbows on his knees and his hands pressed together. The electricity went out more often now and the air turned a fluid, pristine shade of black, against which he was a muddy smudge.

In the dark he took hold of her and covered her mouth and for the first time through the war she felt the pulse of real terror. It was not only her, it was bigger than her: he was wringing shut the light of the world. When he is gone from here, there will be nothing left. She struggled and resisted but she was weaker than she knew and with all that he ate now his gravity was strong; she felt she was pinned at the bottom of an ocean. This pit that he was had grown as big as a continent.

She hid in the corner of the bedroom for a very long time. She'd thought that perhaps she could pry him open. If what he was in his being was twisted and shunted, a clot against the natural passage of light, then perhaps once inside him she could break something loose, but when it came down to it she was small and afraid. It was too much for her, she thought—this knowledge she carried. Who was she but another anonymous bystander? She thought of the old woman with her soup and her photograph and she wept as the woman had wept, and for hours. Had the woman gone away, like most of her neighbors? Had the soldier in his jealousy gone and killed her? She wept, and that was the last of her feeling; after that, she grew very dry.

She did try to strangle him—he lay sleeping in the blackness. But he threw her off and began to laugh.

The next day was long. He went out for food but came back with nothing and he paced the apartment in a state of anxiety. There was a haze in the sky and a faint smell of smoke, and this was the day the tanks rolled in. She and the soldier were equally astounded, for though everyone knew of the tanks' existence, they'd not been seen through the war in this part of the city. They rolled down the street in a column of five, thick-skinned and faceless, with hard angles. They rolled over the blockade at the end of the street, crushing the heap of bricks and doors and chairs and lumber as if it were all just a pile of twigs. The streets went silent and the buildings lowered their eyes.

Later there were footsteps down the hall and then came a pounding on every door in succession. A man's deep voice bellowed blurry orders and the soldier took hold of her and covered her mouth. He smelled now of cleaner metal and cleaner dirt and she wanted to believe that this was a sign of redemption, but wasn't sure that such a thing was possible. He held her just then longer than necessary, one arm around her chest, one hand at her mouth, until after the footsteps had faded onto other floors, and only later, in retrospect, as the bombing began, did she see that the moment had been an opportunity, for in this defensive embrace he trembled just a little. He was thinking of something outside of the war, and she almost felt it—a tug of pale pink. Which meant that there was an aperture somewhere. But just as rage had hardened the walls of his veins, so fear had effectively hardened hers. He let her go and she sank into the armchair.

The bombing began then to the south with an awful regularity. The sun was a smooth burning disk against a yellow-gray ground and a false twilight descended upon the apartment. He began to speak and then to rant; he paced and circled and jabbed his finger in her direction, though she knew that she was not the object here. He leaned close to her and whispered and pointed toward the south; then his voice rose and he pointed with yet greater fury. He hurled a glass across the room. Then he picked up a picture frame and pushed it in her face. There was a woman in the picture who looked something like her, in the arms of a man in a dark gray suit. Then to make his point, he hurled the frame.

She tried to dispute this but he was not receptive; his face was as hard and thick as the tank. She felt he needed to keep his wits about him if he hoped to have any effect on this circumstance, but as the bombing came closer, he grew only more frantic. There were islands of flame across the city to the south and helicopters passed overhead in pairs, with a roar that drove out any tentative sentiment. She found a knife in the kitchen and came at him with the thought that at least there was red inside, or what would be red, so long as there was oxygen—if the blood got free of his clothes and the smoke cleared. But he grabbed the knife with a look of irritation and held her hair and held the blade to her throat. He shouted in her face. Perhaps there is no way of understanding, she thought. And a great despair broke open at the thought.

After all that they'd been through, she found, there was nothing she could do for him. He donned his coat and his pack and took up his gun in both hands and departed as abruptly as he had come. The city grew quiet as if in anticipation and she listened to his footsteps fade down the stairs. A moment later he emerged at the front of the building, ran a few steps and—rat-a-tat-tat-tat-tat—he fell. She watched from the window. The sniper was invisible, the street was still.

So that was it, she was free; it happened so quickly. She donned her funeral dress in earnest now and ventured cautiously into the hallway.

The light was gray, the life of the building drained. Many of the doors along the hallway stood ajar and each room was a strange, deserted province in itself. She found high chairs and house plants and jars of pencils, paintings and throw rugs and decorative plates. She found clocks and books and bars of soap and folded laundry and piles of magazines. She found notes pinned up to the doors of cabinets and unopened mail and shopping lists. A few of the doors were splintered around the deadlock and in these rooms the furniture was rudely upended and loose papers blanketed the floor like snow. In one case a sofa was axed to pieces.

She found a table set with two plates and two glasses, though oddly only a single napkin. She found a card game abandoned on a little table with one hand facing up and the other down. She became aware of a tugging, as she'd felt with the soldier— then a pale shade of pink but now a multitude. Indigo, rose, a dry turquoise, lime green. A breeze through grapevines wound on a trellis, a bay horse on a hill. Lavender. Violet. A white china plate on clean white linen. They were flashes, very brief, almost nothing in themselves, like an anomalous two or three frames in a film. The skin of a woman's shoulder in water. Jasmine flowers. A red plastic shovel stuck in the sand.

Then a fantastic crash shook the side of the building. Paintings fell from the wall in the room where she stood and dishes clattered and an easel toppled. She was on the second floor now, in a corner apartment, and when she looked out the window she saw tanks in three directions.

But then a soft and swelling feeling—the streak of a sunrise, empty fields. The flutter of pigeon feathers over cobblestone. Waves crashing. Pine trees. A mango dripping juice onto a slender thigh and a room lit with red light, with a plastic lawn chair. Trying to keep her wits about her, she pushed on down the stairs to the site of the blast. The door to one of the front facing apartments had blown off its hinges and dented the wall. Inside, the exterior wall was gone; the tossed up furniture gaped at the street. A few desultory flames licked at the jagged edges of the wall and a floral curtain fluttered over nothing. There was yelling in the street; she pulled back into the hallway.

This madness, she thought, is getting out of hand. The funeral is over, something more is required. But what? She darted again up the stifling stairs and went closet to closet in the light remaining, though most of what she found was already dead. Out a second floor window she heard a succession of blasts and then a crash and then a terrible howling and when she looked out she saw men in armor, faceless, flung about the street in pieces and a tank that was tilted up and gnarled. She didn't understand, for a moment, what she was looking at. Men spilled out of the tank through clouds of smoke and there were others running up from behind with their machine guns and packs and their desperate protocols, shouting orders and pointing their guns at the windows—and there was a leg there, just lying there, not far from the tank, amid a scattering of other debris and near the leg a helmet and a heap of she knew not what. And howling unabated. Howling, like an animal, from no visible source. Indiscriminate bursts of artillery spewed outward from the panicked knot of activity and soon, overhead, came the roar of a helicopter tethered to the city by a beam of white light that slid and slithered across the tops of the buildings and down over streets and into alleyways in jerky but not uncertain paths, glaring across the panes of high windows before flooding for an instant the scene below.

I must get up from the street, was her only thought. There are *limbs* in the streets. The shapeless heap has *fabric* in it.

She ran into the hallway and up the stairs. The air was hot, with a chemical smell, and she knew she was running out of time. She tore in and out of half a dozen apartments, beset by inexplicable associations—a cactus lit with clear, gold light; a glass of water on a table on a high terrace with greenery—before stumbling upon a well of tranquility: a room with deflated balloons on the walls. A handwritten sign with multicolored letters. To the left, on a sideboard, three quarters of a cake on a plate that was wrapped very snuggly in plastic. And here again—but not here—but in her mind—or somewhere—was the brown haired doll in the yellow dress—and the face of—almost, or not exactly a face but a sense of warmth and a scent. The room hung in the mess of the war like a glass globe ornament. There was a tender feeling of recent departure and she would have wept again if she had anything in her, for behind that doll—there was a woman behind it, and behind this cake, there was a mother there, and she recalled that the world had once been a joyous place.

She found what she was looking for in that apartment, and found it, in the end, by touch and not color, without any real sense of what she actually needed, for night was falling and there was no light that reached as far as the closet. But she felt it, it was silk—real silk—and very thin, like water; it was sheath-like and narrow and a perfect fit.

Of course there were things she would miss, she thought—the shapes of things. The shapes of dahlia flowers, and apples, and pears. The shape of herself with her curves and her lines. She made it up three flights of stairs in complete blackness, holding the plate with the cake in the crook of her arm. But things change, she told herself. We can't go on clinging to illusory scraps. Buildings, being perishable, are shaky icons, and how much more so the body itself? The soldier was dead and his death did not matter in the least.

When she made it to her door, she saw what she had come for: red-orange and gold in the living room window, as bright as anything that ever was. The top corner of the opposite building had been hit; flames leapt up around the torn edges of concrete and up from the broken out windows below, and from the great gash, a column stood in silhouette—flames. A soft action, a licking, a kind of tenderness. It was a lantern held up, the final portal, and looking down now in the light, of course the dress was the same: red-orange and yellow in silhouette, in swirls. She was right, then, all along; she had not lost her bearings. She found her book on the shelf where she'd hidden it and wrote very carefully, in a stately script: *A cylindrical object on fire in the dark.*

Then another blast and she watched the walls actually ripple, which she wouldn't have known was even possible. There was a great deal of noise and she was wading now through an epoch of memories—breasts, knees, shoulders, thighs, a confusion of body parts; a young girl with a cat. A thousand people smiling. Then a blow to the ribs and a bowl of cherries. It was longing, all of it, the human condition, and it would tear her to pieces if she did not get out soon. She lit the burners in the kitchen in case there was anyone left to listen and tried to explain for posterity just what was happening. The building was on fire. Alarms were blaring out of sync from the floors below. She couldn't remember what she'd been instructed to do in a fire. Surely something with water? When she was done with the burners, she drew a bath.

While she waited, she stood and watched the column. Like an angel, she thought, if she'd believed in angels. Like the shape of the idea of an angel. Then, in a rush that filled her with awe and elation, the column collapsed and she knew she was done. She left the water running over the edge of the tub in the hope that it would drain through the floor and offer some protection to those below, particularly the child whose birthday it was, and whose birthday it would go on being. She closed all the windows in the kitchen and took the cake into the bathtub and the blue of the frosting seeped out through the plastic and swirled with the billowing red-orange silk. It was not blood in the end, but silk and water. She'd found something precious, something very important. She'd done all that she had been able to do. She coughed and smoothed down her dress and waited.

My Arrival

There is something—, the woman wrote in blue, then paused. She was perplexed by the nature of these expectations. "My Mommy and Daddy" [photo]. "My Family" [siblings and pets]. Pets? She looked out the window; there were ravens along the electrical line. *When I was young,* she wrote, *I wanted to be a parrot.* But a full reality, every part flush—she struggled to see the connection. *Just fill in the blank.* A line across a pale blue surface. She tried to remember something of childhood: a small, yellow house. Warm grass and insects. The pictures were frozen on shards of glass all loose from gravity and some of them false. She remembered things in photographs taken before she was born; she remembered other people's memories and television commercials. There was no connection, one to the other.

In black, the woman wrote: *It's not as if childhood—.* The little blue speaker crackled and stammered. The child murmured, then began to cry: a shrill, glassy wail coming through the speaker, a faint, fuller echo from the room beyond. She scratched the words out and tried again: *If when you—.* What did she want to say? She watched the speaker, which remained very still. She wrote *you* again and then a period and held the black pen fixed on the period.

*

The child lay on a blanket on the floor, little soft bones and bundled skin. There was a space, from the beginning, around the child's eyes, like the space around the eyes of a blind person. She held a red toy over the child's face. The house around her was very quiet and still. She held a blue toy and let it dangle. Nothing. She lay back on the carpet and looked at the ceiling.

There was a kind of disjunction she had not been prepared for. Important things had come disconnected. She held the red toy and the blue toy up in different hands toward the ceiling, then threw the blue toy against the window. The way the *child's* body seemed cut loose from everything, a restless weather beneath its skin, motion without action. She wanted to say that she was up for this. When in the moments of the child's birth, moments of damp white cotton and vinyl surfaces, when the space dis-jointed into squares that sounds fell into, disconnected, with the drugs that she told them she hadn't wanted—when God opened up for her the truth of the world and she lay there in it alone, split to the root with the mutual, much bigger aloneness of God touching down to her deepest part. She felt space all around her, then as now, at the very moment when space should have contracted completely. There was this *space* was what she thought she should write. "My Arrival" [about me when I was born]. There was this *space*—she wanted to write it in white, but only against a pure white surface. And I saw that even God was alone.

*

She told the man when he came home that she thought the child was blind.

He isn't blind, the man said. How do you know, she said. He began to explain to her what she already knew and she threw the dish towel onto the floor. *I read the books*, she said. She lay on the sofa and watched the black plastic frame around the edge of the television, which was something that calmed her. It gave her and the man a way to share the same room. The child fell asleep flat on the man's chest, so small that she thought the man's hand would crush it.

"My Mommy and Daddy" [photo]. She thought that perhaps she should draw a graph. She spent hours the next morning sitting at the computer, calibrating the colors and ratios. In the end it was a pie graph: 20%, 52%, 28%; purple, green, and lem-on yellow. She thought she'd hit on something important. She taped it into the space marked [photo].

*

There were moments of a feeling like crumbling apart and moments of a feeling like swelling with liquid. She wanted to get this down but the words were dead under the scratch of the pen and she could only think of stillborn babies. She had become a kind of prophet.

There was nothing to get down though, exactly. She knew in calm moments what it was. But not all moments were calm.

She wrote over and over across one page: it is not as if—.

*

One day, the neighbor came to the door, holding a pie tin with three pieces in it. The woman took it as a sign that God was watching her. The neighbor said: I heard the baby crying, I thought you could use some company.

She decided to stop thinking of the things that passed as *days* and to think of them instead as *colors*. Sunlight, darkness, sunlight, darkness, clouds. Yellow, blue-black, yellow, blue-black, gray. One day it rained, so that would be gray with a kind of silver glisten. Not everyone, she knew, would have seen it this way; the neighbor would surely have said the day was clear: clear being not a color but a condition allowing for other colors. But she saw the tint of yellow everywhere now and knew its relation to *day* to be somehow pivotal. The average person saw very little in the world. The man saw only what was right in front of him and had to do with something he needed. She didn't blame him for this. She no longer considered herself much like other people.

The neighbor came again some colors later. She said: I stayed home with my babies too, it's the right thing to do. All these

women who think they can do everything. What babies need is
to be held and talked to.

*

The silence became a presence in the house, a thing that followed
her and sat with her, and she wondered if this was the form of
God. She thought about God more and more these days, no
longer afraid that He was inside her thoughts. She had no idea a
house could be so quiet. At the office, she'd been surrounded by
voices; they flowed over and between the low, upholstered walls,
in and out of the cubicles. She liked to think of herself at work
as a boulder in the stream of all these voices and needs. She
designed newsletters and advertisements, managed the website
and oversaw the production of annual reports—there was no
one else in the company who could do these things, or there
hadn't been. Now that she'd left, there was another woman.

She tried turning on the television, then the radio, then both,
but they did nothing to dispel the silence. She muted the television and imagined the silence as an old bearded man in a robe
on the love seat. She watched the frame around the picture and
then watched the reflection of the window across it until the sun
passed and the reflection disappeared, and then she watched the
frame again.

*

One color—a flat, dull yellow without any vibration—she wept
throughout the afternoon. A storm rolled into the valley that
she'd become and beat so hard that even she was alarmed. She
searched for crevices in which to shelter herself; voices came at
her from all directions. When the man came home he found her
curled very small beneath a table in the nursery and he was concerned and tried to touch her but the touch failed to penetrate.
The storm had passed by then, she was vacant and still. She told
him she was wrapped in layers of cotton padding. He brought
the child from the crib and sat with her on the floor and in her
weakened state and her deep confusion she couldn't determine

which of them was right: him for believing he held the child or she for believing that it was impossible.

*

She made another graph: a line graph. The horizontal axis she configured in thousands, the vertical axis in single units. She chose three colors—red, black, and green—and plugged in numbers as seemed appropriate to the color. Red: five, two, seven, four, three, one. Black: three, eight, nine, seven, five, two, two. Green: ten, two, five, one, eight, five. The lines darted up and down, in and out of unison. She took great satisfaction in their slender, jagged motion, their freedom in darting up and down, and in the space they held open between them.

"My Arrival" [picture of me at hospital]. "My Arrival" [about my name]. She made a bar graph, and then a pie graph with seven wedges instead of three. Then she made a bar graph with cylinders. She sized them to fit and printed them out and taped them into the blanks. "My Arrival" [birth certificate]. "My Arrival" [cards & gifts]. She made seven graphs for [cards & gifts] because there were several pages to fill.

*

When the pastor spoke, his voice sailed above her, the words blurred together, smooth and rhythmic. She watched the light that fell across the altar and glow of the altar cloth beneath the light. With what she now knew of God, she thought differently of church. As a child, she'd believed that the glow of the windows was the glow of God's love in a palpable form, but she suspected now that light was something different. She didn't know exactly what light was. But she knew, at least, that the windows were manufactured, and the glow was the result of the colors in the glass, in shapes that were fixed by slender cords of metal: just as the Bible was made all of words. What use on earth did God have for words? God knew well enough, she could only expect, to cede to men who spoke with loud voices and broad, sweeping motions of the arm. The chapel was a room that belonged to the pastor. Perhaps the basement was the room that belonged to God, with its long empty tables and carts of folding chairs. She imagined God sitting on the counter in the kitchen in the basement with the old deaf woman who prepared the coffee.

*

She rose one pink color saying yes! yes! yes!, believing this all to be a spell she had the power to break. She'd dreamt of something involving trees and sunlight and a young man who wanted to do her a favor. She couldn't remember exactly. The young man touched her shoulder and there was a sense of fullness.

She would try, this color, to talk to the child. She'd read in the books that words were important, like food. *You wouldn't deprive your child of food, would you?* No, of course not. She smiled when the man went off to work. She waved down the street and held the child against her chest. She waved to the neighbor. She pulled several dead blossoms from the bush beside the door, thinking: see? see? it's not difficult. She would talk to the child. *This is a flower bush. This is a door knob.* She didn't know exactly what to say.

The child lay on the changing table, all skin and belly and flapping limbs, like a bug. What a strange immobility, she thought. She tried to say it out loud, thinking she might as well start with the words in her head. But they weren't words, she discovered, so much as breezes, largely translucent and loose around the edges, and when she tried to say *what a strange immobility* her voice sounded to her ears very weak and pale, hardly there at all. The immobility of un-concerted motion, was what she was thinking. To be moving all the time and not move at all. She brought the computer to the nursery and made a bar graph in which all the bars were horizontal. The child began to cry, wriggling and flapping on the changing table. She didn't know if the air was too cold or too warm. She fed the child and the child fell asleep.

*

She sat alone with the pastor in his beige-green office, having left the child with the mothers who gather daily in the basement. He had a kindness that was more like the shape of kindness than it was the thing itself, which was something that she respected. She felt calm today and like she knew a great deal, like she could see who she was from compassionate heights.

He said: You had some trouble last week.

She said: Yes.

He asked if she wanted to talk about it. She said: A storm came through. I was there just sitting, watching the storm from the rocks. He said: A storm, that's interesting. He nodded and seemed to ponder the term. Do you have any idea how this storm came about?

She said she didn't know how weather came about. He said: Oh, various conditions. There are bound to be conditions. She said: I was holding the child and it didn't touch me.

He began to tell her what she already knew. She said: I know that already, I read the books. What I mean is that what the child's skin was wasn't reaching me.

But you were holding the child? You had the child in your arms?

I tried to break through but I couldn't.

He looked at her with the shape of kindness, which she imagined to be something like a hexagon. He said: You were feeding the child? You held the child in your arms? She said: I tried to feed it, but there was this other layer. There's this padding everywhere. There's no connection. What layer? he asked. She laid her hand across her belly. I'm afraid, she said, that the milk isn't mine.

She felt calm inside but she began to cry. She said: The child exists very far away.

He smiled at her from across his desk. He spoke and his voice flowed gently over her. She cried for a while and then returned to the basement and sat with the mothers who were drinking coffee.

*

The child cried through the afternoon. She tried to talk but her voice was lost in the sound. She told herself that she would remain optimistic. She would not cry. Perhaps what she needed were stronger words, more structure. She put the child in the bobbing seat and set it on the floor and began to read aloud from the dictionary.

Bellwether, she read. Noun. One that serves as a leader or as a leading indicator of future trends. Bellwort. Noun. Any of various perennial plants of the genus *Uvularia* in the lily family, native to eastern North America and having solitary, nodding, yellow bell-shaped flowers. (I've never heard of a bellwort, she said aloud.) Belly. Noun. See abdomen. The underside of the body of certain vertebrates, such as snakes and fish. Informal: the stomach. An appetite for food. The womb; the uterus. A deep, hollow interior: *the belly of a ship*.

The child cried and cried and after a while slept.

*

There was a color—gray—in which she didn't get up. She never told the man. It was a dark gray color, with brown in it, with a beige luminance around the edges. The sheets were sour and limp and dark. There were sounds—she could hear them—very far off, but the much closer silence held her limbs all pinned down. There was a collusion, she saw, between the stillness and the silence. If the silence was God—? It was all quite confusing. She felt very, very still in the cave of the bed, like even time grew still, even the wind and the clouds, and like she couldn't remember what movement felt like. She knew there were things she needed to do, and doing required motion, but she couldn't move. It was very low, she knew, but not entirely uncomfortable.

She felt around in the stillness for God. She wanted God to know that she was beginning to understand. She wanted to lay a hand on God's shoulder.

It was noon before a crack appeared in the shell of stillness. She needed to use the bathroom. In three or four steps, she broke the outer layer and was then flooded with fear at a pitch she'd never known. She tore across the landing to the nursery. *God God God God God*, she thought. The child was crying and wriggling, flapping its limbs. She held the child to her chest and sank to the floor, shaking.

*

She sat with the pastor in the beige-green room. She said: I was thinking about the shapes in the stained glass windows. The windows, he said, yes, they're very beautiful. Do you know who made them? she asked. They were made many years ago. She said: I was thinking about the metal lines between the shapes.

He smiled gently.

Do you see God, she asked, when you're giving your sermons? Do you think that He's out there in the audience somewhere? He said: God is everywhere, God is all things. She said: I don't think that God has much to do with noise. Or with the color in the windows. Or with books. He said: The Bible is the word of God. She said: When I see God He is usually off in a corner. I see him only from the corner of my eye. God is love, the pastor said. God is our refuge and strength, a very present help in trouble. *Therefore will not we fear, though the earth be removed, and though the mountains be carried into the midst of the sea.*

She pondered this. She said: I read to the child but the child doesn't listen. I try to talk to the child, but the child's ears are very small. He said: That isn't necessarily an indication. She said:

121

I know. She looked out the window to where the leaves of a tree were tipping and tilting in the light.

*

"Welcome Home" [a picture of my homecoming]. "Welcome Home" [the world around me when I was born]. She made a graph with three-dimensional bars, and another whose bars were subdivided: 23%/44%/33%; 10%/72%/18%; 49%/4%/47%; 12%/39%/27%. The terms of the activity grew ever more complicated, as if by some organic evolution. She made a graph whose horizontal axis was labeled by letter—A, B, C, D, E, F, G, H—and whose vertical axis read in the tens of thousands. "Welcome Home" [about going home]. She made another with letters in no particular order: G, L, P, R Z, X (horizontal); D, E, H, R, Y, P, Q, J, U, I, A, S, C (vertical). She explored a more nuanced palette of colors. She made one graph using only shades of pink, another that shifted in twelve gradations from blue to purple to red. She was filled with a sense of possibility when she worked. For every graph that she made, ten more sprang to mind.

"Welcome Home" [a picture of my first home]. "Welcome Home" [the cost of living when I was born].

For every "Watch Me Grow" she made a pie graph. "Watch Me Grow" [weight & height by month]. "Watch Me Grow" [doctor visits]. "Watch Me Grow" [favorite foods and eating habits]. "Watch Me Grow" [vaccination records]. "Watch Me Grow" [childhood illness records]. "Watch Me Grow" [sleeping habits]. "Watch Me Grow" [dates my teeth appeared]. "Watch Me Grow" [funny first pictures]. "Watch Me Grow" [favorite games and friends]. "Watch Me Grow" [photo—look at me in the tub!].

*

She wasn't sure if she should tell the pastor what she knew. If he's speaking for God, she thought, he should get it right. But she didn't want to hurt his feelings. He'd studied many years to be a pastor. He'd wanted to be a pastor since he was a child. He'd told a story in a sermon once about playing baseball with his grandfather when he was very young and later being told that his grandfather died. Because of this he became a pastor. She tried to broach the subject gently.

She said: When I was in the hospital, there was a nurse who seemed very kind and considerate but then later I realized she spoke like that to everyone. She was a good person, he said. No, she said, it was only the way that she used words. She was a deceitful person? No, I don't think so. The pastor listened expectantly. She said: The nurse had a yellow barrette to hold her hair back and there was a moment in the middle of all the contractions when I saw her standing in the doorway with her foot in the door and she was adjusting her barrette and looking at something out in the hallway, even though here in the room a child was being born.

That's interesting, the pastor said. She saw that it would be no use. She liked the pastor, she wanted to feel that they understood each other. Wherever we are, she said, there is a doorway like that doorway. That is what I want to tell you. Even in a room where a child is being born.

*

There was a hummingbird outside the kitchen window in the morning, with a scarlet red breast that flashed in the light. The woman stood holding a dish towel and watched. It bobbed and zipped about the fringes of the hydrangea, dipping with precision into the pale blue blossoms. It paused in the air every three or four sips, so full of motion it was intensely still, hanging in the air like a comma, or a period. The woman was struck with a sense of poignant confusion.

*

She tried to work on her graphs but it was difficult to focus. She made only one, the day of the hummingbird: a pie graph using only shades of red, of which there were twelve gradations available: 12%, 2%, 7%, 15%, 9%, 11%, 4%, 6%, 14%, 12%, 7%, 1%. She printed it large and taped it across a two page spread. "My First Outing" [about my first trips out]. "My First Outing" [photo of me out and about].

She was so tired. She was like a zombie walking, no sensation in her limbs, thoughts like big, soft blocks with no edges or texture. But she fed the child, sitting in the rocker, propping the pillow under her arm. Sleep overcame her and she dozed involuntarily. In the tangled space of dream-thought she saw—or felt—or tasted—or heard—the red of the hummingbird, the smallness. Little swallows of sweet blue liquid. She snapped awake with a feeling like falling from a ledge.

The child was watching her. It startled her: watching. He was not blind. He had blue eyes. He was sucking rhythmically and watching her. There was a calm curiosity. He knew her. He watched her as though he were asking her a question.

CPSIA information can be obtained
at www.ICGtesting.com
Printed in the USA
LVOW12*2117150218
566781LV00002B/17/P